CW01239459

First published in 2025

Meet Me at St Brelade

©Copyright 2025 Sophie Holland

ALL RIGHTS RESERVED

No part of this publication may be reproduced, stored in a retrieval system, or transmitted, in any form or by any means, electronic, mechanical, photocopying, recording or otherwise, without the express written permission of the author.

Printed by AMAZON

Meet Me At St Brelade

Written by
Sophie Holland

A love story of destiny

Dedication

Mom and Dad - This one is for you!

Parents are more than just two people, who bring you into the world. Together in marriage you have worked together to be the best parents, a daughter could ask for.

A mother is someone who nurtures you,

watches you grow and

helps you achieve.

A father is loyal; crack's the dad jokes, and someone who you go to when things are broken and need fixing. You just know dad will sort it!

I'm lucky and very fortunate to have parents of gold.

Thank you for being my parents

Love you always

Sophie

x

Chapter One

Prologue

One year earlier ....

Sitting on the sandy shores of Portsalon Beach, better known as Ballymastocker Strand in the magical country where the luck of the shamrock, traditional music and a pint of Guinness is all but gentle nods to the mystical country that is Ireland. Finley looked around at the breathtaking landscape that fringed the coastline's perimeter. Taking a deep breath in and exhaling all his worries, he took pen to paper to write down his feelings, if his family continued to disagree with his career path, now was a better time than any to break free and discover what the universe had planned. Opening his heart, he poured almost every emotion he felt through his strong, Irish blood onto a piece of paper.

Finley or Finn as he preferred was from a town called Donegal, in Ireland, he was the brother to four younger sisters and his horse-breeding parents Mary and Patrick. Finn's father was known as the owner of

Ireland's leading thoroughbred stud farm and had a glowing reputation within the horse breeding industry. Despite having grown up and spent most of his childhood with horses, Finn's heart belonged to the ocean and to be frank he would have exchanged a horse for the thrill of a surfboard without a moment's hesitation. Having spent hours studying for his final exams, he found himself about to graduate from university with what he thought he wanted more than anything- a degree, which was very much now going to be a scroll of paper, a certificate to be framed to go on the wall, if you will. With spring waving its goodbye and the sight of the first blooms, luscious green grass and mesmerising blue skies, summer was all but a hop, skip and jump away.

Taking a deep breath he, stuffed the piece of paper into his empty drinking bottle and screwed the cap on tightly. Clenching his knuckles until they turned pearly white and shaking his head, he paused momentarily, before throwing the bottle into the foamy, washed sea. Finn then turned his back, and walked away, working his way back to the public footpath.

Little did he know, where that bottle would resurface.

Chapter Two

I woke to the most beautiful sunlight, shimmering between the floral curtains framing my bedroom's old, single-panel glass window. The warmth from that very sun could be felt all around the room. Summer was greeting me with its presence, growing more profound each day. Jumping out of bed to draw back my curtains and open my window allowing the fresh air to fill my room. I hopped back in bed, snuggled into my freshly washed sheets and reached over to pick up my journal.

My journal was a space to be completely open with my thoughts, feelings and daily gratitude log. I also added a to-do list on each page at the bottom left corner. If I don't write it down, the task won't get completed, not for the lack of not wanting, it's just my mind gets cluttered with, well, life, I guess. Besides, nothing is quite as satisfying as crossing each task off and looking at a completed list.

Today's to-dos were simple as it was my day off from work and involved, house chores, posting out my preloved clothes to include some new pieces, I had sold on an auction site. Surely, I can't be the only person who buys clothes just because they are a good price in the clearance sale yet fails to wear them. I also had a hair appointment and planned to meet my friend

Zoe, at St Brelade Beach afterwards. A plan of ease yet, one I was completely looking forward to.

Since having moved to Jersey five years ago, I have managed to create the most wonderful life for myself. I've moved house twice. My first property was a small two-bed apartment in the small, yet thriving town of St Helier, it was the perfect get-go for me and provided me with the security and grounding I needed to begin essentially my new life on the island. I managed to make friends, establish connections and hold down two jobs.

During the last year, I have moved to the most idyllic dreamy one-bed fisherman's cottage, nestled in the peaceful and scrumptious parish of St Brelade. The cottage was owned by two elderly Jersey residents, who in all fairness had allowed the cottage to see better days. In fact, it wasn't even advertised to let, I happened to be exploring the island and scrambled upon the property, in the woodlands. Admittedly I will confess now, that one credential of my personality is tending to be a little nosey. Not in an annoying glass-to-wall sense, more curious if anything. I just had to look in the windows of this quaint, stone cottage. The garden was more of a small jungle with towering grass and uneven ground. Yet, inside was what only could aesthetically be described as cottage core on the highest level possible. The fireplace was crooked and central to the living room, the walls were neutral with old artwork gently resting upon them. The floor was deep mahogany oak, each panel unique and well-worn. I recall, my heart flooding with love and sadness, how could this magnificent jewel on the bay, be left unloved?

This was the point when I heard a gentleman's voice asking if he could be of assistance to me. Smiling and paying the weather a compliment, the man looked stern with a rich Jersey tan and furrowed eyebrows. He was calm and polite yet got to the point that I was on his land. I recall apologising yet, in the moment whilst I was reached backwards, I happened to stumble and land on my bottom. The gentleman assisted me with his hand and still looked at me like I was some creature washed up on the shore. Once again, I apologised and turned to walk away, yet before I fully turned, I managed to ask the man if the cottage would ever be a home again. Once more, he looked at me, yet this time a slight smile emerged. We spent a good hour talking about how the cottage was once his mother's before she passed away, he said he and his family already had a farmhouse in St Ouen, so therefore had little use for the property. Years had passed and apart from stripping it of its belongings, donating most, the bricks continued to stand still in time. He mentioned he visits the cottage every few months, and always fixes a wreath on the door for the holiday season but chooses not to go inside. The pain was too raw, as his mother adored the little cottage. I remember seeing the hurt in his eyes, yet I felt so heart wrenchingly sorry for this cottage I had stumbled across. This was when I plucked up the courage to ask if he would consider renting it to me. The old man looked at me like I was bonkers, but I told him I would turn the cottage around and make it a home. He expressed it needed work and the garden for one was a complete and utter mess. I told him, I would spend my evenings working on it.

During that conversation, there was an element of trust and desire that sealed the deal. I guess the fire in my eyes was my ticket to this cottage becoming mine. The old gentleman had agreed to rent me the cottage on one condition, he didn't want any form of payable rent for the first six months, and after that time, he would make his final decision on renting it to me long-term.

The weeks passed that summer and I spent just about every possible free hour touching up the cottage here and there. Structurally the cottage was fine, so after replastering the walls, a fresh lick of paint and some handy work, it was habitable in just under four weeks. Then I made the task to turn habitable into a home. My home. The renovation work as I call it was enjoyable, with having to save every penny I allowed myself to believe that it would be mine. Whether that was wishful thinking or motivationally inspiring, it gave me the spring in my step that I needed.

Leaning out of my window and listening to the faint humming of cars passing by, coupled with cheers of laughter and shrieks from beachgoers, not to forget to give a nod of recognition to the gardeners cutting the welcoming manicured lawns. I could see the sea twinkling and glistening against the beams of sunlight that rested upon the surface. The reflective light glistened like diamonds encrusted on a piece of fine jewellery. Each wave competing to be the best in show. The bay was magic… pure magic.

To stay on Jersey, I had to work harder than in any previous job I had. There were times after long days, I truthfully questioned why I was working endless hours to essentially survive month by month. The wages were decent enough on the Island, but the cost of living was high, even reducing my groceries from branded to non-branded made very little difference. For now, all my thoughts and worries, I wasn't putting away savings each month for my future, just to wake up and smell the salty air and being on the Island of Jersey was the greatest gift. Speaking honestly Jersey had given me the reward of what living was all about, for every tear and overdraft entry each month, it was worth it, just to look out towards the ocean and feel my heart beating through the wall of my chest.

Chapter Three

'So how are you honey?' questioned Kyle.

'Oh, you know Kyle, busy as always, what about you?'

'I'm the same, my chair feels like a never-ending revolver,' he chuckled.

'That's good though, I did wonder why I hadn't seen you propping up the bar at Murphy's on a Saturday night,' I giggled.

'You know, I haven't stepped foot in Murphy's for around a month, my feet can't handle standing a minute longer than they need to. Epsom salt bath and a large glass of fizz for me know, whilst scrolling through my socials, equals pure bliss'.

'That's still a great Saturday,' I smiled.

'Do you still like Jacob from behind the bar?' queried Kyle.

'No, no, I've heard these rumours flying around, Jacobs just a friend, he helped do the panelling in my cottage, that's all'.

'

'Hmm… if you say so, I've seen the way he looks at you'.

'You're imagining scenarios Kyle, your mind is delusional,' we both laughed.

Jacob and I were just friends, that's the truth of it. When I moved to the island, I didn't know anybody, it was nerve wracking not knowing where places were. That's in a roundabout way, how I met Jacob. It was my first weekend in Jersey and I was staying in town at a small bed and breakfast, before I signed my first lease. There was a board outside Murphy's with its specials displayed, I was drawn in by the seafood platter, trust me I will never forget the taste of those freshly caught, succulent, juicy prawns, smothered in sweet mayonnaise - chilli sauce. Jacob was the barman, that rainy February day, and let's say we hit it off straight away and Jacob is still one of my strongest friendships I have on Jersey.

'So how am I styling this blow-dry for you today?' Kyle asked while running his fingers through my wild, slightly heat damaged mane.

'I need bounce', I shrugged.

'Bouncy blowout it is then! I think you need to book in for some highlights soon, get your summer beach look on form'.

'Kyle, I arrived on the island a mousy brunette, you've turned me into a golden goddess.'

'You look so good though, look at your tan, you picked it up from the beach or have you been hitting the bottle?'

'Don't be so cheeky, no self-tan would create this deep of a tan, trust me I tried nearly every brand when I lived on the mainland, but I'm always in the garden, it's my haven.'

'You are for sure a golden goddess, in your grandma era', he laughed whilst flicking my hair in his round brush.

'Oh, shut up, gardening is good for the soul. I think that whole grandma cliché has gone when it comes to gardening. The garden allows me to think, to be clear, to be free,' I stuttered whilst pondering on each word.

'You are serious, aren't you? I'm only playing with you girlfriend, if you're in your grandma era, then I'm in my grandpa era, the balcony on my apartment is looking like a float from the Battle of Flowers'.

'Watering commitment must be huge', I laughed.

'Don't be stupid, artificial dear, Jersey indoor market, to the left of the fountain, you will find Sheila, best silk flowers on the island. Nobody can tell, I even find myself on the daily standing with my watering can, obviously pretending to water the plants, immersed deep, in the down but two apartments chit chats. Ha, you don't need to buy your weekly copy of Bonjour, let me tell you. Got all the gossip I need', he blurted, whilst pointing with the brush and not remotely attending to my hair.

'I don't think I could do artificial plants; I like the reward of growing something from seed, watching the different stages.'

'You forget the part, where you need to get on your hands and knees and weed the borders, treat the plants for diseases then pull them out when they die.'

'Kyle, you need to try it!'

'I'm good, these fingernails need to be kept clean, I'll stick to Sheila, if you want a discount say, I sent you to her'.

'Come on, focus on the task in hand, I have so much to do on my day off, to include attending to my garden,' we both burst into fits of laughter.

Kyle was for sure, crazy, eccentric and spoke exactly as he found fitting, with his strong Glaswegian accent. I applauded his honesty and his kindness, he always showed me such warmth and from being a customer, we were now very good friends. There was no topic of conversation off limit, Kyle was that guy every girl needed in their friendship group.

'

'Hairspray?' he tapped the can.

'Best do,' I nodded.

From a cloudy horizon of hair spray, I emerged from my chair, looking if I so say so myself, amazing. Kyle had magic fingers. I always felt incredible after visiting the salon, my hair for sure had soaked up all the hair oils and goodness from the hair mask. The sea often made it dry, so the tender loving care from Kyle, was always a treat.

'That's thirty-eight pounds for today, tap when your ready', he smiled.

With a tap of my debit card, I turned to Kyle, 'You best book me in for those highlights, text me my appointment and I'll add it to my diary later. If we can do them on your late night that's better for me.'

'Right you are, see you probably at the weekend, that's if you haven't taken up sowing in that grandma era of yours', he smiled smugly.

'I don't think it's advisable I answer that, us Grandma's have can have a wicked sense of humour you know, later baby.'

Walking out the salon I felt like a new woman, only one-word springs to mind and that would be fresh. I happened to agree with Kyle my hair did need a root touch up, trying to maintain this look of a beach goddess was indeed very hard. Although I thrived on the effortless chic buns it provided. Somehow, the mix of golden tones, softened by the taupe caramelised root growth, just looked expensive. Old money I think they call it, or so I've read. Come to think of it, my wardrobe was very much inspired by an old money look, for I lived in high waisted Ralph's and a cable knit jumper could for sure be found assembled around my shoulders, which I must point out needed some after sun lotion promptly.

Chapter Four

Walking down the uneven, cobbled side streets of St Helier back towards my car, I stopped off at my favourite, world renowned chocolatier. For not only did I fancy a Pistachio latte, I couldn't help but pick out six delectable chocolates from their renowned selector packs. I adored the shop and found myself in there weekly to pick up a sweet treat which was usually for the weekend, but despite it being a weekday, I caved into my sweet tooth and that inner voice saying, 'go in'.

'Hi, what can I get for you?' smiled the assistant.

'Can I get a large, Pistachio latte, one shot, oat milk to go please?' I smiled whilst reeling off my mammoth tick list to the perfect order.

'Sure thing, help yourself to our new honeycomb maple tart, they are new in'.

'You don't have to ask me twice, what pack do you recommend? I'm more of a milk chocolate, desert style girl.'

'Oh, you need to try the sticky toffee and clotted cream bomb, they are divine,' pointed the assistant.

'I will take a pack of those for me and a pack of the new honeycomb too for my friend, were catching up later,' I added.

'You might as well do the deal then and get a third pack', she insisted.

'Okay well, we will get a mixed assortment'.

The lady packed up my chocolates and popped them in a paper carrier bag and smiled whilst passing me my drink and a napkin.

'Would you mind if I had a spare paper bag from you?' The assistant was most obliging, As I exited the shop, I rested my latte upon one of the outdoor tables and lifted the lid to give it a little stir. To me there is nothing quite worse than having the syrup all sticky at the bottom of the cup. I needed to taste all the yummy, nuttiness possible. I also added the mixed selection pack to a separate bag and shut the lid back firmly on my latte, trapping in the rich coffee bean aroma. To the left of me there was a public bench in the centre of the street, with an elderly lady seated resting her legs. I walked over and handed her the carrier which had inside the mixed selection box.

'Hi, I'm Bobby, here's a box of chocolates for you, I always try once a month to do a random act of kindness and gift a stranger, some flowers or some chocolates.'

'For me? You know, I haven't been brought chocolates in years. That is so very kind, and to do that as a monthly gesture is just so lovely.'

'I figured out the world needs more kindness, plus there is nothing more rewarding than putting a smile on someone's face,' I nodded.

'Sit down dear, before that drink spills,' she pointed.

'I guess, I can stop for a few minutes. It's my day off and I have everything to do.'

'I wish I could remember what that feels like,' she smiled, and her eyes gleamed.

'Must be nice though know, to have the time to enjoy the island,' I noted.

'Did you say your name was Bobby, I'm Agnes by the way. I don't get out a great deal. It's a lot for my legs to catch the bus and carry groceries. I do make the effort once a week though. I take a rest here once I'm done. I love to watch people go by, whether there working or shopping. I could sit here all afternoon.'

'I love to people watch too, except I hide behind my sunglasses on the beach and do it there,' I laughed.

'Explains your tan, although I detect an accent, you're not a Jersey girl, are you?'

'No, I moved here a while ago from the mainland.'

'Do you have your own house?'

'I do. I have a cottage at St Brelade. It's very small and quaint. It's quite magical if you ask me. The walls are filled with my personality and many a trinket. I collect just about everything from soft toys, to porcelain dolls and books.'

'How lovely, I love to read too, classics are my favourite.'

'Oh yes, I have a few leatherbound classics of my own, my favourite must be Black Beauty and The Secret Garden. I honestly can't choose between the two. What about you?'

'Great Expectations', she said without a moment's hesitation.

The conversation was flowing, and I found myself with a shallow inch of coffee at the bottom of my cup, which had cooled considerably since I had begun it. I could have talked all afternoon to this kind and gentle lady. I was confident she was in her late eighties, perfectly curled hair, and pink dress with dots, her weathered features radiated her happiness of being present in the conversation. One could only assume, she didn't have much in terms of socialisation as she was for sure, living on every word I said.

In a weird, yet wonderful way I had struck up what felt like a friendship. I felt obliged and wanted very much to know more about her.

'How are you getting home?'

'I will get the green bus at half past.'

'I know you have only just met me and as bizarre as this sounds, I would love to give you a ride home. It's getting quite warm, allow me to carry your shopping?'

'Bobby, I would be eternally grateful, I was dreading walking this up the hill', she said, whilst pointing to her groceries.

'Come on then, pass me those, I'm only across the street, I touched lucky on the pay and display,' I smiled.

Agnes was every inch a kind and gentle soul, she was warm and interesting to talk to. I saw both joy and sadness in her emerald, green eyes and I sensed she was lonely at heart. Despite having errands coming out of my ears, I didn't feel fazed to stop and spare my time to help this lady. I was if anything extremely glad to have made someone's day and help at the same time.

'Nice car', she winked.

'A classic', I laughed and winked back. That's exactly what my car was, a cream, vintage convertible from the nineties. Admittedly she'd undergone a paintjob, but she was perfection for driving round the island.

'Where to?'

'I live very close to Portelet Bay', she waved.

'So now you tell me, we have been neighbours for all this time, and we haven't met.'

Portelet Bay, was situated on the south-west of the island. A treasure of a beach, despite the mammoth task of the concrete steps to get to it. Not so bad going down to the beach, but horrendous climb back up, unless your extremely fit. I have tried to count the steps but can confirm on several occasions I have always found myself loosing count. I've been informed its around two hundred and twenty yet, I'm still to verify this knowledge, but I'd say its pretty much accurate.

I like to think of Portelet bay as my thinking spot. Whenever, I have felt homesick or a little overwhelmed, I felt the beach offered much comfort which was overly warming with a tight embrace that keeps giving. There had been many a time, that I needed to be sat on this very beach, not that I had suffered anxiety, it was more of the fact I didn't know what my future entailed on the island. The rugged, bespoke rocks that melted into the curves of the bay, felt safe, secure and solid. I must add also, that if one wants to tan, this beach I can confirm provides the deepest, rich golden-brown tones your skin will soak up. I'm not sure how a beach can make a difference to your tan but trust me when I tell you there is definitely some form of sorcery takes place there. Without a shadow of a doubt, it's a tan to envy and you would find it hard to gain a better shade of golden delicious from a mediterranean island.

'The traffic is light for this hour of the day,' I noted.

'Yes, it is quiet, are you sure you don't mind giving me a lift?' said Agnes.

'I'm more than sure Agnes, let's get you home and you can enjoy the afternoon sunshine,' I smiled.

'I'm looking forward to having tea and a scone in my garden', she chuckled. My heart filled with happiness, and I couldn't help but smile on the journey. Agnes was very talkative, and I hardly got a word within the conversation walls. To see Agnes waving her hands around and laughing and talking with all sorts of expressions was enough fuel to keep me smiling. I felt so glad to have met such a charming lady. The short journey sailed quickly and before we both knew it, we were pulling into the driveway of Agnes' bungalow.

'This is your home?' I questioned whilst flapping my eyelids in disbelief.

'Yes, I've lived in this bungalow since I was a girl, and do you know? Once upon a time it was my grandparent's property, it then became my fathers and when I married my husband, Joe bless his soul, we both lived here. I never had children of my own, otherwise I'm sure by now it would be there's. A beautiful bungalow, my home.'

'It's magnificent!' I smiled.

I was completely shocked at how beautiful Agnes' bungalow was, she had kept it very well maintained from the front with the mobility additions to the entrance of the door.

'Let me help you with your shopping and I'll get out of your hair,' I insisted.

'Thank you, Bobby, that's kind'.

The bungalow's well-kept appearance mirrored the inside too, if the walls could talk then I could tell they would have a tale or two to tell. The warm, sunshine yellow walls were filled with wooden and metal photo frames of all shapes and sizes.

'Pop the kettle on will you Bobby, and pass me a scone, you are welcome to join me if you will?'

Looking through the archway into the lounge, I saw her rocking chair near the central part of the room, in front of the television. A table to her side with a

'

newspaper and a mug of what looked like contained cold coffee. Nestled around her were cabinets filled with trinkets and charms. Everything and anything from porcelain fairies, thimbles of the different Jersey parishes and even a sand castle flag or two. The home was washed with love and adorned with memories of a lifetime. Agnes lifetime.

'Agnes, I'd love to stop for a scone and cup of tea with you.'

The next forty minutes sailed by and both Agnes and I, quite literally put the world to rights. We talked just about everything and anything from how Jersey had changed right through to Agnes' crochet hobby. We had left no stone unturned or as so the saying goes. Not to forget the famous yet highly debatable conversation of what goes first. Jam or cream. I felt an element of guilt for no apparent reason when it came to saying good-bye to Agnes. I left her with my telephone number and my address and told her I would stop by when I could. I told her she could call upon me anytime. Within those couple of hours of meeting Agnes, I had made a new friendship, which I felt could very much blossom in time.

Chapter Five

'Why have you not picked up', screamed Zoe.

'If I told you, I doubt you would believe me', I stuttered.

'Oh, please tell me you pulled some hunky surfer dude?' Zoe pleaded.

'Quite the opposite in every way, shape and form', I giggled.

'This I need to hear! I don't think we will get a spot at St Brelade, its packed. Let's go fishing instead,' Zoe insisted.

'Catch of the day... a hunky, blonde with an olive tan?' I added.

'Girl, you read my mind. Let's go to St. Ouen and have a coffee and fish.'

'Right you are, meet you at the bunkers, and I want extra salt and vinegar on mine. I will fill you in on my very interesting day.'

At that Zoe put the phone down. Zoe and I had such a solid friendship, I find it hard to believe we are not blood related as she is more of a sister to me than a bestie. We had our own language which we had formed when it came to scouring the opposite sex. Just to clarify I'm not a maneater even if I sound like one. When I talk to Zoe, it's just harmless banter. I do think it's fair to say that there is no harm in scouring the talent that live around the waters of Jersey. Afterall, I don't know about you, but I was brought up under the illusion from watching far too many fairy tale movies, that we all have a prince charming out there, we just have to make our own fairytale journey, which I might as well point out is going more south sailing for myself. Maybe I'm just too picky when it comes to guys, but I know what ticks my boxes and trust me when I say I have a lot of boxes to be filled.

Both Zoe and I loved to spend many an afternoon or Sunday morning drooling over the local talent at the beach. However, I must point out we were solely interested in a specific male species, they needed to be beachy. Allow me to explain that term a little more. If they are not wearing a wet suit, don't have the attributes of a deep tan, golden shaggy hair and a surfboard then they can keep walking. There was something about a surfer that tickled both our hearts and made us weak at the knees.

I quickly pulled up at my cottage, raced in the kitchen to swap my comfy trainers to my trusty wedges and changed my t-shirt for a polka dot bandeau number. One tip I learnt from going to the beach was to always wear a strapless number because tan lines just stand out in a non-attractive way. They scream look at me I got a tan, you know what I'm referring to, a school nostalgia vibe, when you're in the changing rooms after spring break and you are all comparing tan lines. Grabbing two bottles of icy cold water and a share bag of salt and vinegar crisps, I had secured our starters. Not to forget the chocolates which luckily hadn't melted thanks to Agnes allowing me to pop them in her fridge. I always carried my book in my bag, which would usually be the latest read on the store shelves. I was very much a bookworm and heavily followed upcoming releases and would always circle and note the release date of a novel I had to read. I wasn't a huge fan of non-fiction books, but I had acquired some books about Jersey and the history of the island from a local charity shop.

Jersey during the Second World War, was the only part of the British Isles to be occupied by German forces. To this very day, Jersey still celebrates the day the island was liberated on May 9th. The impact of the German occupation on the island remains raw and visually tourists would expect to see a bunker or two scattered all over the island. St Ouen has a bunker, which I always find myself walking around whenever I do a power walk along the five-mile road. I always get the most eerie of feelings around there. To think once upon a lifetime ago, troops would have been working there, guarding the bay, which we now surf and relax upon. I find the history of the island fascinating, an island which suffered and was tortured by the opposition, yet today stands proud in all its unspoilt glory. To see those bunkers and landmarks gives me pride to think what the island has achieved and to this very day continues to achieve, priding itself as the beating heart of the British Isles. I feel proud to call Jersey my home, to be living on this island filled my lungs with the vital oxygen I needed to not only keep me alive but to feed me with all the happiness and smiles this place had already given me.

Chapter Six

'Your hair looks so good', exclaimed Zoe.

'I don't think you will say the same after I've been in the sea.' I replied.

'Throw it up when you go in the water, but leave it down for now, one o'clock, is reeling you in on his line honey.'

'Shut up, I've only just got here, let's get a drink from the café', I laughed.

'Oh, I don't think so, the fishing wire is pulling you in, closer, closer, and caught….' stuttered Zoe. I tried to frown to make sense of here muttering rubbish she was spitting out, and I had grasped that Mr One o'clock was making a bee line towards me.

'Hey, I'm Corbin, I haven't seen you around the café before'.

'Hi, I'm Bobby, and this is my friend Zoe. We normally use the café, across the way, but seeing as we've come to top up our tan's we thought we would sit here, quite the suntrap.'

'Oh cool, do you surf ?' he smiled.

'I do, but I haven't brought my board with me. We

'had planned on going to St Brelade but it's packed.'

'I own the surf hut, so if you want to hit the waves, I'm your guy,' Corbin smirked whilst flashing his icy white teeth, which gleamed against his deep, olive skin. I couldn't help but blush, Corbin was very easy on the eye.

Corbin was good looking for sure, he was ticking most the boxes and owning the surf hut was a huge tick, he was extremely well groomed, with the perfect definition of a beach body. I even noticed Zoe was nodding her head and beaming from ear to ear.

'That's a kind offer but I'm not exactly prepped to ride the waves today, I have no wetsuit with me,' I hesitated, hoping he would turn and walk away.

'No sweat, come with me, you too Zoe, we have drinks at the hut,' he insisted whilst pointing the direction to the hut.

Before I knew it Zoe was flinging my beach bag over her arm and twirling her hair around her fingers whilst cooing over Corbin. Little to my amazement, I found myself walking alongside Corbin for the next, one hundred and fifty yards or so. The hut was brimming with surf boards and wetsuits of all different shapes and sizes, complete with changing rooms and a fridge stocked with just about every cold drink you could think of. The hut had a small crowd outside of surfers catching up and talking.

'So, this is your business?' cheered Zoe.

'Yeah, for the last five years, I love the ocean. I'm not the kind of guy you would find behind a desk and on a computer,' he nodded.

'That's cool though, to find a job you love,' I added.

From the corner of my eye, I happened to notice a tall guy, with golden hair and a wetsuit approaching the hut. I raised a half smile from the corner of my mouth, as he became closer.

'Choppy out there today boss, I think we should call a warning for advanced only', he said to Corbin, whilst detaching his safety cord from around his board.

'Right, you are Finn', said Corbin.

'Advanced I am not, so that's me out', I eagerly pleaded.

'What about you Zoe?' Corbin questioned.

'Advanced with a capital A', gloated Zoe, whilst gazing into Corbin's eyes. I couldn't read Corbin's facial expression, but I felt he was wishing I was the advanced one he was taking out on the waves.

'Let's get you a board and a wetsuit, meet me down the beach, I'll be waiting for you', he replied.

'

Corbin nodded at me whilst flashing his teeth once again, he grabbed his surfboard, a bottle of icy cold water and tapped my shoulder before heading down the steps towards the beach.

'He is cuteeeeeee,' squealed Zoe.

'I think your going to have a fun surf session', I insisted, whilst not drawing in on Zoe's instant admiration for Corbin.

'How do I look?' she questioned.

'Like you are going to ride the waves of St Ouen', I laughed.

'Bobby I was meaning do I look hot?' Zoe corrected me.

'Yes, but play it cool Zoe, don't put your eggs all in one basket'.

'Shut up Bobby, I am filling my basket full of eggs, he's so hot, did you see his six pack?' she gloated.

'It was hard not to miss Zoe, he had his wetsuit around his waist.'

'I best not keep him waiting, I know this was supposed to be some bestie time, but…'she hesitated. 'Steak is Infront of my eyes', she screeched whilst jumping up and down on the spot.

'Zoe, just go and be the peppercorn sauce to your steak,' I added whilst pushing her towards the beach steps. Zoe walked towards the steps with a grin from ear to ear. In all honesty, I didn't mind the fact I had been deserted as so to say, I had my book, and the rays of sunshine were beaming down on me. That's when I remembered, I needed to get a drink. Seeing as I was stood outside the surf hut and having noticed they sold drinks there, I decided to walk over.

'Did you not fancy the water today?' smiled the guy who seemed to be Corbin's right-hand man.

'No, I'm not that good of a surfer. I enjoy being out there but I'm still a little hesitant,' I smiled.

'You're best to be sensible, you can never predict the waves. I'm Finn by the way, local surf instructor as you have probably guessed', he said warmly.

'Nice to meet you Finn, the local surf instructor,' I cooed in a sarcastic tone. 'I'm Bobby, very much a surf amateur, pleased to make your acquaintance'. Finn laughed and held out his hand.

'Can I get you a drink?' he questioned.

'That would be amazing, even though its crazily warm. Can I get a weak latte?' I asked.

'Coming right up', said Finn as he unzipped his wetsuit to his waist almost mimicking Corbin's appearance. I wasn't sure where to look, and I felt my cheeks flush with warmth. Finn's body was even more chiselled than Corbin's. As for his tan, it was a piece of artwork, he was a piece of artwork. I tried not to stare at him whilst he had his back turned towards the coffee machine. I needed to act cool and be the opposite to Zoe as I didn't want to draw to much attention to myself admiring his features.

'There you go, there is a biscuit on the side, please tell me you are not one of these calorie counting ladies', he added.

'Thanks, and no I'm not', I smiled.

'Good, can't deal with girls that can't eat this and that, not that you're a girl. I mean you are a girl…err woman. Lady that's what I meant to say, lady', he exclaimed bashfully in his sexy voice.

I must admit to watch Finn, squirm his way out of that explanation had made my heart sink. There was something about the way his skin flushed under his caramelised skin, not to mention his accent, how could I not mention his sexy, Irish accent. I think his accent just topped off his persona to perfection. I don't know about you, but I'm a complete sucker for an accent, especially if its Irish. The light tone to his voice with the rugged edges of his strong but not overpowering accent melted me to complete and utter mush.

'That made you go quite red', I giggled.

'Yeah, got me a bit flustered under the collar there', he nodded.

'So, I detect from your accent you're not from Jersey originally?'

'I'll give you a ten for your observation'.

'Sorry', I paused.

'Why are you apologising, I was just winding you up. The answer to your question is no, I'm not Jersey born. I've not been here all that long. I moved to Jersey for a fresh start, a change. Life just got heavy and weighted on me. I didn't want to go to a big city such as London. I heard good things about Jersey, and had you not guessed by my job, I love the ocean,' he explained whilst resting his water wrinkled, hands on the counter. There was something about the way he talked, the calmness in his voice. I felt his gaze was reaching into my soul and every word I attentively listened to. I didn't know at this point what had come over me.

'I think Jersey was a good call for you'.

'I think so, Corbin has been amazing, offering me a job upon observation of the way I was surfing on the bay.'

'No way, some interview hey.'

'

'I hadn't been on the island a week and I landed a job, which at that time was probably the biggest blessing I could have had.'

'Totally. A surf instructor must be a pretty cool job.'

'I love the ocean, it's the therapy I needed after college,' he said bashfully.

'I'm a huge believer in fate', I added.

'Me too', he said whilst winking which made my inside melt even more. I knew that response was aimed toward me, or at least my heart told my mind just that.

'So, you've heard about my magnet to the island, tell me yours? What drew you to Jersey?'

'How do you know I'm not from Jersey?'

'Well, I detect a twang in your accent too, yet I did question myself before asking, as you defiantly have the signature Jersey uniformed tan.'

'Well, you guessed right, I'm from the mainland but I grew old of it too. Somehow, despite only being young, I fell out of love with my home, the surroundings. I fell out of love with England. I wanted a challenge and an adventure. Jersey has given me both.'

'How long have you been here for?' he questioned.

'Five years,' I replied.

'Long time then, so you must be settled, have lots of friends, a boyfriend?' he questioned in a very cheeky way. I admired though the way he added the bf tag to the end of the question.

'No boyfriend, but plenty of friends,' I answered watching the side of his mouth rise at the corner smugly. 'I had a bumpy start on the island, and I did at one point think that the cost to live here was obscene, but I didn't want to go back, I worked just about every hour to survive', I explained.

'I feel you, Jersey is bloody expensive'.

'I see it as an investment.'

'What do you mean?' he questioned.

'As children were taught to save pennies in a piggy bank, as teens we pay not intention and spend it. Then we become adults and adulting is scary when all these bills appear, so we learn to save again for our future. Well, I see Jersey as an investment on a personal scale. The island doesn't create me an interest rate for a nest egg for the future, but it rewards me with a life, a lifestyle,' I paused before continuing, noticing Finn was devoting his sole attention to me. 'I wake up every day smiling when I look out my window and I see the ocean and the sun rising. I'm rewarded with beauty, and a feeling that makes me burst from inside. I will never leave Jersey; my heart belongs here.'

'

'I believe mine does to', said Finn whilst touching my hand.

'Sorry, I got lost in thought', I blushed.

'Stop apologising Bobby. Ireland will always be my roots. These arms are made of the finest Irish blood…'

'Don't forget your charm'…' I giggled.

'Well, you can't put a price on being in the presence of a beautiful lady, so yeah, I guess, I must flash the Irish charm. However, I do see Jersey as my future, something in the water here is magic.'

'I agree, and you have the luck of the Irish on your side.'

'That is a true saying you know.'

'I'm sure it is', I nodded, whilst noticing Zoe running toward me from the distance.

'Did you see me out there?' squealed Zoe.

I suddenly had to tell a slight porky here, as in all truthfulness I had spent Zoe's surf time, locked eyes with Finn, and if I'm honest with my heart pounding from inside, I could easily have spent Zoe's surf time locking lips with him. I felt as though I had been lured into an ancient Irish spell of magic, because I had struck the pot of gold and followed no rainbow to find it. Finn was a fresh of breath air, I found myself hooked and drawn into whatever spell he had conjured over me in the brief time we had met.

'You were amazing, how did you get so good?'

'Bobby, I wasn't amazing, I kept falling on purpose to feel Corbin's muscular arms around my waist', she said informatively.

'I know that I'm just you know, playing a long, keeping it cool.'

'Oh, I see, the Irish one made you week at the knees?'

'Shhhhh.....' I tapped Zoe's arms.

'Cute, very cute....'

'I said shhhh', I giggled.

'Here's my number Zoe, maybe we could catch up some time if you fancy it?' said Corbin, whilst placing a kiss on Zoe's cheek.

'Okay, I'll text you later', she cooed.

'Nice to meet you Bobby, I hope Finn kept you company', Corbin added.

Looking at Finn, I smiled as he began serving some guys, 'Thanks for the drink, I had a great time.'

I turned to Zoe, and gestured to make our way to the car, I wanted to say goodbye to Finn, but he looked

'

busy, and I didn't want to come across as too keen and I guess scary. Zoe and I continued to walk toward the car park, that was until I heard my name being called from the distance.

'Bobby, it was good talking to you, I must go, I have a lesson out on the ocean. See you around maybe,' he smiled whilst placing a screwed-up piece of paper in my hand and squeezing it before letting go. I presumed it was his number, so I stuffed it in my pocket safe, and I guessed I could drop him a message later. I was bursting inside with happiness.

'So, I take it we both caught the catch of the day?' screamed Zoe.

'I think you could say that', I said gently whilst watching Finn run back to the hut.

'I know we didn't get to spend much time together today, but it was fun.'

'Yeah, it was,' I added.

'Do you want to come to mine for Pizza?' asked Zoe.

'I think, I'm just going to go back home, catch the last few rays and watch the sun go down, maybe we could go for pizza in the week?' I offered.

'It's a date.'

I drove down the five-mile road, barely speaking, just looking at the long road Infront of me. The air was warm, yet the cool breeze made me my skin tingle all over. Zoe had her head down and her fingers tapping away on her phone, evidently, she was texting Corbin. I could tell by the smug smile on her face and the way she was wiggling her toes in the passenger seat.

Zoe lived only a few minutes away from the bay, so the journey to her apartment was quick albeit very quiet.

'Call you in the morning', she said with her head still firmly down and devoted to her phone.

'Okay boo, catch you later,' I said whilst blowing an air kiss, which lingered in the air until Zoe finally looked up and caught it.

I turned my head back toward the direction of the hut, wanting with every inch of me to open the screwed-up paper, but I chose to let the suspense await me until I got home. I already was planning my evening texting Finn subconsciously in my mind. Grinning from ear to ear, before driving away, I grabbed my smartphone and placed an order for Pizza, a Caesar salad and of course a portion of chocolate cake, from the best pizzeria located on the seafront of St Brelade. If you know, you know. Known by its renowned brand name, it delivered above and beyond, with each visit. I intended on having some Jersey ice cream with my 'chocolate cake which was currently chilling in the freezer.

Chapter Seven

I was grateful to be back at my little cottage, just in time for the evening sunset. I scrambled out a plate and some cutlery and made a balancing act to the outdoor wooden table. Admittedly, the table had seen better days and desperately needed some wood treatment, yet another thing to add to my to do list, but for now it had continued to serve its purpose. Walking back inside the cottage towards the fridge, I pulled out the bottle of wine which contained the remanence from the previous night. I didn't drink daily, but there were some nights where a soft drink just didn't cut the edge. Tonight was one of those evenings.

Seated at the creaky table, I devoured my pizza and tilted my full glass towards the golden hour sunlight. The warmth from the sun was healing to my skin and the view always amazed me. I treasured this part of the day and nearly daily spent this segment of the day looking out towards the ocean. My mind often decompressing the day or sometimes just looking out wondering what lurked beyond the eye, where the sea met the sky at the horizon. The waves glistening gently with the occasional ferry insight. The ocean delivered a calmness to my soul, and the thought of having its absence in my life filled me with dread. I couldn't imagine not waking up or saying goodnight to the ocean. Looking down at my plate which was filled with the remainders of pizza crusts and the occasional drizzle of sauce, my eye kept flickering towards the screwed-up piece of paper. I needed to know what the contents entailed even though the thought made me scared. I had this thought eating away at me that it might not be Finn's number. Ever the optimist, I spent the next ten minutes refraining from opening the note and devoured my sole attention to sundown.

I moved away my plate and cutlery and opened another bottle of wine, it would have been rude not too and I barely noticed the remainder of the other bottle go down. The sunlight had now dimmed so I brought out the matches and lit the few candles which were littered over the table. I loved to read outside by candlelight with waves crashing against the rocks as background music. Now was a better time than any so I took one last glance at the ocean, and with all my heart hoped that the note contained those digits I so desperately wanted to punch into my phone. I hadn't stopped thinking about Finn, since I had left the beach, if I'm completely honest, my stomach was in knots. I kept convincing myself that Finn was a nice guy, but that was all, a mere stranger in essence that had been washed upon the shore. A creature that for a moment had stolen my mind, my thoughts……my heart. The whole 'love at first sight' quote now made perfect sense to me.

I unravelled the screwed-up note and began to read it.

> "May the meaning of this hour be fulfilled."
> —an old irish blessing....
>
> don't look it up to understand the meaning ...just believe in hope and the luck of the irish x

'

My heart was pounding from inside my chest wall, as I read each line, the thumping feeling became harder and more intense. The last line made the inner corner of my top lip rise, into a sort of half smile. I imagined his Irish accent reading those lines to me, which sent me giddy with desire. The back of the note contained his mobile number. I was left wondering why I was being blessed with an old Irish blessing, but under Finn's strict instructions I refrained from looking up the inner meaning to the words.

I flipped the paper note over and added Finn's number to my contact list, whilst adding three kisses at the end. Momentarily staring at his name, I removed two kisses and kept it to just one, before pressing save. I wanted to text him immediately, but I was hesitant. Unlike Zoe, I was a little shy when it came to dating. I also didn't want to come across as over keen and scare Finn away as much as I knew I needed to message him.

I gazed out to the water, not really thinking about anything. Just staring at the beauty, the bay offered. I always was amazed how each day I noted something I hadn't seen before. Jersey was really a never-ending gift. My heart adored the island. Jersey was an unspoilt secret island, which left me despite being here a while still wanting to discover and unturn every rock I passed.

I chose to stay seated outside, and lost track of time. The calming acoustic soundtrack of the waves was relaxing from what had been a very unexpected day. A day, I feel I will never forget. I didn't want the day to end, I had my very own waves of flutters in my stomach glistening with excitement.

'Oh, what the hell', I sighed. I grabbed my phone and caved into my reservations of wanting to be seen as an overkeen love interest. My thumbs and fingers performed and little dance upon the keyboard, whilst I thought of what to say. I paused smiling at my phone before typing.

Today was cool....

No Bobby, you don't want the day to have been cool. Think girl...Think! I slowly erased those words.

Consider the hour fulfilled...maybe we should continue to explore the meaning x

Yes Bobby, sexy and saucy yet, keeps me from looking like an eager beaver. That text is gold. Before I could back track on what I had just typed I hit send and threw my phone on the table, whilst swigging the dregs of my glass. My heart was even pounding deeper than before. Why was I feeling such intense emotions? I've met and talked to loads of guys over the years, I was for sure a socialiser. Yet, today was different. He was different. I wanted to know more about him and see his kind face again.

I was determined not to overthink the text, so I turned my phone off and left it in the kitchen cupboard. I didn't want to torment myself. Today had been a long day. I switched the light out and called it a night, after a quick crisp, cold shower. Today had been overwhelming to say the least.

Chapter Eight

After what I can officially confirm was the worst night's sleep, I opened one eye shallowly allowing the morning island sun to awaken my inner soul. Seeing the sun shining always made me smile, it was the daily dose of medicine which allowed life just to be that little more extra. I reached out and tapped my hand on my bedside table feeling for my phone. Then I remembered. Finn. I recalled leaving my phone in the kitchen drawer after sending that short and sweet text. I tossed and turned most the night thinking about my encounter with Finn, whilst clock watching most of the night. I pulled back the duvet which was all lumpy and bumpy from having threw it off and on me during the night, pushed my toes into my slippers whilst noting I needed to book in for a pedi. I felt the soft lilac shade on my toes, needed a refresh, into a punchy, summer sunset coral.

Hobbling into the kitchen, whilst securing my slipper. I flicked the switch on the kettle, reached for my trusty mug which If I told you was a Christmas mug, would make you roll your eyes with madness, but there was something about this mug, it made your tea taste better. Don't ask me how, or what sorcery is involved its just a fact. Tea just tasted better out of my Santa

'

mug. Besides I only have my girlfriends see my mug collection, evidently, they haven't sent me to the crazy yard, just yet.

'Come on phone, turn on', I whispered. Whilst tapping my fingernails onto the screen. I was convinced at the point the back screen light came on there would be a ping come through. Finn for sure would text me back. I felt the connection, and the crumpled note said as much as so. A minute went by, and I had checked my screen a million times and toggled the aeroplane mode on and off. The ping from Finn was surely, making its way down the non-existent phone cord.

Bam there it was, I breathed a sigh of relief because for a moment I had convinced myself I had been left out to dry, but by the looks of the text icon and his name a lit on my screen he had very much text me.

'So, you want to fulfil the hour… Ask me no questions, just say you will be there, 6.40 tonight. Meet me at St Brelade.'

I couldn't help but grin from ear to ear. I even found myself jumping up and down like some fourteen-year-old, getting asked out by her high school crush. I was beyond excited though. There was something about yesterday, about Finn, that just felt so right. I didn't want to jinx things, but he was just so perfect, he ticked every box.

However, before 6.40pm was due to roll around, I had a hefty day infront of me. I had not only a mountain of admin tasks to do, but I also needed to tend to the garden and make myself look irresistible. The way I looked at this moment in time, trust me when I tell you, I needed a lot of attention.

First things first, another strong brew was required, followed by some dunking cookies. In my opinion my regimented packet of cookies was my pre – breakfast. There was nothing better than a dunked cookie of sweet goodness. Most mornings weather permitting, I would take my cup of tea outside and stand bear foot on the garden, I believed in the hype of grounding. There was something calming about taking small footsteps across the dampened grass. Connecting our souls to this beautiful planet.

Before moving to Jersey my life had been hectic, and time was just passing before eyes. The days rolled into weeks and the weeks rolled into months and before I knew it Easter had unfolded, and Fall was waving hello enveloping my eyes in amber toned leaves. There were times when I lived on the mainland, I look back and I realised just how much of my life I lost. I didn't live life to the full. I allowed the daily nitty gritty to get in the way. My life was just passing through time. However, Jersey put a stop to all that. Within a few days of being on the island, I felt such a magnitude of gratification, for what I had received from the island. When I say received, I'm not even talking about ornamental things. I'm talking about the spirit of the people, the happiness from the sunshine, the warm rain which touched your skin like a kiss from nature. A simple walk on the beach to find shells, of all shapes and sizes. The island had taken hold of my heart almost immediately. Jersey took me from a lost girl needing direction to a woman of eternal gratitude. That's the only way I can explain it.

That's where the grounding comes into life, the morning session of connecting my body with the earth, also allowed me to become the ever-keen gardener that I was. When I say gardener, I'm not an expert, I'm very much an amateur, but in my mind, I felt like a pro. That's surely what counts. I had spent my evenings, reading books about planting flowers, and propagating seedlings. I had learnt and developed a wealth of new knowledge, I walked around the garden checking my flowers, pruning here and there and fixing bamboo cane supports to my climbers. I loved it, I loved the surprise of seeing a flower open. The journey of seed to flower always amazed me. I felt so lucky to have this cottage, to have this cute cottage garden filled with grasses and florals, set with the backdrop of the sea blending into the sky. I knew I was lucky and there wasn't a day that went by, I didn't show my gratification to the island. In all honesty, I think I will always be in some from of debt to the island, because however much I thanked it, it would never be enough. Jersey was the gift, that kept on giving.

I was excited to meet Finn later. I spent a moment thinking about how to do my hair, curly, tight curled, loose barrels, half up half down, a simple ponytail with some cute claw clips. Then there was my outfit to plan. I wasn't exactly dressed to impress and get his rich Irish blood warm under his collar. I wanted to make an impression. I wanted him to want me, on every level, everything from my body, to my mind, to my soul. I wanted him to feel the way I felt.

I hoped in the shower, which turned into an everything shower, even the ambree de vanille honey body polish came out. Trust me that's giving as the price point on that tub is extremely spenny. With silky smooth skin, I smothered my body in an express self-tan- just to erase any tan lines I had from my bikini, If I looked good, I knew I would feel good. With an express four-hour tan you can't go wrong, not that I reached for the self-tan much with the Jersey sun. Somehow the Jersey sun had a way of developing my skin with a golden tone, with spending very little time bathing. The sun was always hiding in the clouds and just being in shorts or going on daily walks the sun just tanned you. I was lucky to have the jersey tan, most tourists crave when they visit. Trust me, the deepness and tones beats any European tan.

Dressed in a short linen playsuit, my body let's say was left to marinate. I left my hair soaking up some hair oil, as it didn't need washing, the curls were still looking good albeit a little looser and softer from my blowout. I grabbed my laptop and placed it on the table outback. The sun hadn't reached the paved terrace area of the garden, it was very much shady and cool. Before getting to work I needed to eat, I was ravenous.

The cookies had left me craving even more of a sweet tooth, so I decided to create a smoothie bowl, fuelled of goodness. Luckily the freezer was stocked with frozen blueberries, strawberries and raspberries. I had an over ripe avocado which I halved and fridged the remainder. I then added a banana for an extra sticky sweetness. I loved smoothie bowls, for breakfast. I think I had been heavily influenced by socials for making the prettiest smoothie bowl known to man.

At that point my favourite anthem ringtone leapt itself into action.

'So, guess who is currently sat sipping on an espresso down at St Ouen?' squealed Zoe.

'Seriously, you're joking right?' I exclaimed.

'No, I'm totes serious. Corbin and I text last night, like the whole night, no exaggeration. So, I thought I'd surprise him this morning at the beach,' she panted.

'Zoe, I'm in full support of your need to see Corbin's perfectly chiselled abs, but don't you think you look a bit…. desperate', I paused.

'Maybe, but there is no way I'm letting any other kitty catch that mouse. I couldn't care what I look like. I want him. He is mine,' she added.

'Well, my input is clearly not going to stop you', I added.

'Not on this occasion boo. So, tell me how is Mr Irish?' she questioned.

'I'm sure you can let me know how he is considering you're the one down the bay.'

'I see him, he is already riding the waves. Someone must book an early morning class. You know that's what you need to do. Book a session'.

'Definitely not,' I prompted.

'Come on it would be so much fun'.

'No. Besides, I have a date with Finn later. I say date, we have arranged to meet later at St Brelade.'

'Cute! Oh shoot, I need to go, Toodles.'

'Bye Zoe,' I laughed.

In all fairness, I admired Zoe's ambition and drive, I don't think I could ever be so bold. In my head I could probably manifest the perfect meeting and scenario situation with Finn. I was looking forward to our meeting later. I much preferred the traditional approach of having a time, date and venue. I liked to prep for these kind of things, mentally and visually. This is where I noted to myself my tan was developing just fine.

I attacked my emails and admin tasks with a vengeful attitude. I had created a plan of attack. I needed to work quickly and efficiently so I wacked some house anthems on and allowed my fingertips to dance upon my keyboard, whilst noting I needed a fresh splash of polished on my overdue manicured hands. I wasn't what you would call overly high maintenance, but I liked to look as polish and put together as I could be. The garden, however, was tragic for my hands. Even with gloves, my polish would always chip. The mammoth task which in reality is all but five minutes always seems so lengthy and longwinded, for them to simply chip the following or even same day.

With the sun beaming through the minimal cloud coverage which in essence looked like candy floss waves across the salty, sapphire, blue sky. I plodded on with my work schedule, allowing the hours to roll and unravel the day. Mixed with a feeling of excitement and anticipation of the evening that awaited me.

Chapter Nine

There was something in the air that day which melted slowly into the evening sunlight. I couldn't put my finger on what or why it felt different, but I can tell you it did. My stomach had been doing back flips and cartwheels all day, feeling as though an acrobat was performing inside of me. I have always been told that nerves are a good thing, they give you that rush of power and provide adrenalin that you need. I chose to believe in that knowledge and exercise the fact, in all fairness I had no choice. I wanted to feel calm and collected. I was looking forward to the evening, to see Finn, to learn more about this guy who had overtaken my mind and quite possibly my heart.

I had spent around an hour getting myself ready, a swim in the tub, overloaded with soapy lavender suds and a drenching of my favourite, strawberry kiss body yoghurt, left me smelling divine. I left my hair to do its thing, I wanted the effortless look, so with a little sea salt spray thanks to the sea of St Brelade and a fishtail plait, I had been left with a gentle wave running though the strands. I wanted to keep my look as relaxed as my hair, after all the vibe of the evening was beachy. I chose an oatmeal gipsy, crinkle skirt and

'

a halter neck in a similar shade, which was decorated with shells, which I had hand stitched onto it. This top had to be one of my favourites. I had worn it so much, but it never got old or tired, it just hugged my skin in all the right places. I felt a confidence in the outfit, and I felt having that extra boost would only bring me a little more luck. Not that I needed luck after all, luck was clearly on my side as Finn had found his way into my life. My very own Irish lucky charm.

With my bag handle around my wrist and my flip flops resting on my feet, I locked my car door and made the way down the semi-steep steps to the beach. I chose not to walk to the beach; I didn't need the hassle of a blister or two. The chilled breeze washed over me with its salty tang hitting my eyes. The closer I was to the sea, the deeper inner peace I felt. The car park was so very quiet and despite maybe a handful at most people. I knew Finn and I would have the bay to ourselves.

There he was waving at me in a kind of embarrassing way I wont lie, his cute, over enthusiasm won me over in an instant and I could help but giggle at the sight.

'Over here', he called in that accent which made me go instantly weak at the knees.

'Wow, this looks beautiful', I noted.

Finn was sat on the beach on a checkered picnic blanket, a bottle of sparkle, which rested gently next to 'a bowl of deep red strawberries and melted chocolate dip.

'I brought a bottle, but I wasn't sure what your tipple of choice is, so I have a few beers in the basket,' he added.

'I will probably take a beer later, for now it would be rude not to have some bubbles with those strawberries.'

Finn looked so good, in every essence of the word, he was wearing a pale lemon t-shirt made by the popular surfing brand, which hugged his muscular arms in the right places and a pair of denim ripped shorts.

'You smell incredible,' he pulled me in and kissed my cheek softly which made me want more.

Finn gently poured two glasses of bubbles, and we clinked glasses, 'To golden hour', he winked.

'To golden hour', I repeated.

'I'm glad you came; I had this dreaded thought niggling its way into the back of my skull. I kept telling myself, you would be here. I didn't know if I had partly scared you with my Irish memes.'

'Are you crazy? Of course I would be here. I've looked forward all day to it. As for your Irish charm, it's kind of rubbing off on me.'

'

'Is that so?' he smirked.

'You know I have always had a thing for an Irish accent'.

Finn was laughing and slightly blushing, 'Tell me what is it that makes women so attracted to it?'

'I said I, not women', I raised my brow.

'I'm not being smug here, but it's a known fact.'

'So, what you're saying is I should consider myself very honoured to be in your company.'

'Indeed', he laughed.

'Ha, you are full of charm you know? And to answer your question, I think it's just the tone and how words sound. I like it.'

'Well, at least we cleared that up, now tell me more about you? Why are you single?'

'Just am', I noted.

'A recent break up?' he questioned.

'Nope'.

'A casual thing?' he questioned again,

'No', I shook my head.

'Why then?' he pushed.

'I haven't had the time. Which I know sounds crazy and pathetic because only yesterday morning you came into my life.'

'I'm glad I did', Finn butted in.

'I think I've just spent time living, prioritising myself. I think they call it self-love. I once read that it's best to learn to love yourself before letting a person in.'

'I like that Bobby, you can't love anyone if you don't love yourself, and as for me what's not to love, I can surf, I can scuba dive….' he laughed whilst I nudged him with my elbow.

'Seriously I get you, probably more than I'm letting on', he added.

'Now you can explain, seeing as you made me!'

'Well, it wasn't a spare of the moment thing, my decision to leave Ireland. I had everything a lad could wish for. It didn't matter what exams I passed, or what my ambitions were. I was always seen as the guy to take over his father's horse breeding business.'

'So, you were, what going to be a farrier?'

'I probably would have gone that route and set up my own business, but it all felt a bit much. I don't want to patronise here as I'm all for playing on words or taking the Michael, but I think a guy needs to be a guy and he needs to find his own path in life. I think for women it 'can be different. I felt the pressure to follow suit, but I didn't want to just be shielded by a business. I love horses Bobby, I've been riding since I could walk, but I didn't want to run the horse business. I wanted to see what the world had in store for me,' said Finn with so much emotion and empathy.

'I get it,' I added.

'You do? Because my father didn't. I left Ireland on a bad note with my family. We haven't spoken much since I left. The weight of disappointment is just hanging over me you know. No matter how much I surf, run, walk…. My mind is well you know.'

'Oh Finn'.

'Sorry, what a morbid tool I sound.'

'No, you're not morbid. I prefer your honesty, I think it's good you're talking about it.'

'First time I have since being here on the island, thanks for listening, not exactly first date talk is it?' he grunted.

'First date?' I blushed.

'That's what I'm calling it', he squeezed my hand.

I felt my cheeks blush, Finn had shown me a side of him, I hadn't seen. I agree it's not the topic for first date conversation, but I didn't care. I was happy that

Finn was comfortable talking about his personal feelings. I don't think you get that on a first date usually. Surely if anything it was good sign. I couldn't help but feel sorry for Finn. On the outside he had portrayed a semi- cocky, smug man with a body to go giddy over. Yet the interior didn't match his exterior, he was sad at heart, and I wanted to take that sadness from him. However, nothing I could have done this very evening could have erased it away, for now, I had shown my compassionate side and gained his trust. To me that was an achievement, and I knew, my relationship with Finn wouldn't stay at first base. There was some element of trust and emotion that allowed us to be open.

'Bobby, I want to kiss you', he tugged at my top.

Pulling in towards Finn, I could see deep into his eyes, such hurt and the need to be loved. I wanted to be the person to love him. I fancied him so badly. The kiss was passionate and deep with a hungered desire sealing it.

'So…..' he laughed.

'Fancy a strawberry?' I laughed back, both of us blushing.

'Isn't it beautiful the sunset?' he remarked,

'Oh I know. The sight never gets boring, I love how the sky and sea can't be separated, it all looks as one.

Then you have this huge golden ball beaming across the blue.'

'Yeah, its magic here'.

'It's beautiful', I smiled.

'You're beautiful', he held my hand, and we shared another kiss and toasted the evening sunset.

The evening continued to flourish, and conversation was in abundance. We laughed and cried and laughed some more. Finn even insisted we go for a walk along the sea as it washed against our feet. Being next to Finn, I felt something inside of me, which I hadn't ever experienced before. In a way it was a lightness, the feeling of being carefree and in weird sort of way juvenile. Adult life had paused, and I found myself splashing and kicking water at Finn, not giving a care in the world.

For that evening, I was living on the freshness of the air in my lungs and good company. Nothing mattered that evening, I was just allowed to be myself, in the arms of a hunky Irishman, whom I wanted to call mine. I or should I say we had defiantly made the moment of the hour count. There was no way, I was going to let him slip through my fingers.

'If I'd have known you wanted to go swimming, then I would have brought towels,' he called out whilst throwing me over his shoulder and carrying me back to where was were seated earlier.'

'It wasn't my fault, someone has an addiction to the water,' I added.

'Maybe that could be seen as true. I love the ocean, but I think, I could become addicted to you too', he smiled whilst holding me still in his arms.

'I think I would like that', I breathed faster with each breath.

'Bobby, I haven't had this much fun in a very long time. Especially not with a girl, I mean woman. Sorry,' he looked flustered and quite red the evening sun had kissed his skin.

'It was fun', I smiled.

'So is a second date on the cards?'

'For sure,' I beamed.

Finn passed me a beer, 'May the friendships and relationships you make be those which endure, and all of your grey clouds be small ones for sure.'

'That's beautiful', I paused.

'I guess I needed to say that, be rude not to use my Irish cham, to steal another kiss with you.'

'There was me feeling all flattered, by such beautiful words. Tell me, is that another Irish blessing?'

'Aye, but I added the word relationship, because I don't want a friendship with you. I want to see where this goes…'

Finn's tender words were the perfect closure to the date, apart from him walking me home and saying goodbye with a kiss which was tender, sweet and if I'm allowed to say it pure. Something had taken hold of me this evening, I wasn't the woman I left the house as. I had changed and my intentions had somehow changed. I had everything on this beautiful island of Jersey I could wish for, however tonight though I think I had discovered my need to love and be loved, on a level that goes beyond self-love.

I was ready emotionally and mentally to let someone into my life. That person was to be my very own four-leaf clover. Hard to find and lucky to now call mine.

Chapter Ten

The morning after the night before had me slightly in a tizz, a mare, a frenzy. I was bursting with happiness, and I would be very accurate with my assumption in informing you I slept with a smile which went from ear to ear. I had the most cute and well lovely evening. To sit and talk to Finn on the beach last night was so relaxing and chilled, despite being nervous the evening was completely zen. In a strange way, I felt like I had known Finn a lifetime, yet if the truth be told, I only had scratched the surface on learning all there was to know about this guy who had stolen my heart.

'So, what's the goss?' screamed Zoe.

'No goss, nada', I replied whilst shaking my head.

'So, you're telling me you've been on a date with a hunk that's tick's the boxes and El Punto happened!' squawked Zoe in more disbelief.

'Well, not exactly El Punto', *(El Punto a term we use in our own fabricated language meaning nil)*.

'Go on….', she hesitated.

'We might be seeing each other again, we kissed and agreed that we are both looking for more than just a friendship.'

'That's what you want though? So, it's a good thing. I told you Finn was perfect'.

'I don't recall that conversation, but I agree', I laughed.

'Well, Corbin and I are hanging out all day today, I want to get to see him as much as I can before our course.'

'Oh, that had completely slipped my mind, I really don't want to go off the island for this damn course. Think I could pull a sicky?'

'I don't think it would be worth it, they will just put you on the next course. Besides, we will have fun it's only for a week. We can do some major shopping, flex the plastic,' laughed Zoe.

'You're a bad influence. I don't want my plastic bending. I'm trying to save every morsel I can. This place bleeds me dry. I don't know how you keep up that apartment.'

'That's the benefit of being daddy's little princess'.

'Will he adopt me?' I replied.

'I think after having me, he wouldn't want any more children, especially not another daughter,' said Zoe.

'I need to tell Finn about my trip; he mentioned some sort of surfing party at the weekend. I need to pick up 'some toiletries to travel with. Maybe we can go to town tomorrow if you fancy it?'

'I've already got mine, leftovers from Bali. Are you working today?'

'Yeah, I must swing by the office, and I've got quite a bit of paperwork to do. Still wish I didn't have to go.'

'We will be fine, I suggest you spend every hour you can get with Finn. I need to go; Corbin will be getting up soon?'

'You mean he's at your apartment?'

'He kind of hasn't left!'

'Oh, my days, Zoe you are crazy! I am going before any of your antics rub off on me. Later baby'.

'In a bit', howled Zoe, before ending the call.

Wow Zoe was a real fast mover, I mean next she's going to be telling me she's engaged. I must admit, it worked out well, the prospect of couples dating sounds pretty good, considering were all friends. I couldn't help but worry a little for Zoe, she was an all or nothing kind of person. If I am completely honest, I've had to help mend many a broken heart. I think she just has this desire to have a happy ending, and if she can take a shortcut route to get there she will do. Despite me trying to teach her or educate her on what men are like, she fails to pay any form of attention. Hopefully this time though Corbin could be the right guy. I did think behind his buff exterior he seemed genuine.

Today as mentioned to Zoe, I needed to swing by the office and do some admin tasks. I thought I would do those tasks from the office. As much as I wanted to stay home, I just knew I would end up getting distracted and end up passing the tasks off and sitting in my bed working into the early hours. I loved the flexibility working from home gave me.

I should probably inform you what I do for a living. I work as a admin/secretary/PA call it what you will- for a local law firm. I loved my job. Zoe was a qualified legal secretary, so she had a much better position than me, but I was learning the ropes on the job and loved the opportunities I had. My main task was typing up case notes and letters of correspondence which I enjoyed. Occasionally, I would need to be present in court or be present in meetings. It was rather exciting at times, but overall, I was kind of my own boss. As long as my duties and tasks were completed on time, the company didn't mind where or when or how I went about my work.

Working from home allowed me to choose my own hours, sometimes I found myself waking up as early as five in the morning to get all my tasks done and delivered into the works system, just so I could spend the day at the beach or go exploring. I also once worked from late evening into the early hours just so I could spend the following day at St Malo.

That was one huge advantage of living in Jersey. The mainland was no more than a fifty-minute flight and France was a short crossing on the Condor ferry. I tried to go to St Malo, every few months. The French market was incredible. I adore my cheese, yes, I'm sure you're raising an eyebrow at me. I couldn't agree more, it's the most calorific sport one can be obsessed with eating, but the French do cheese so right.

You step off the boat and all you see is blue and white striped stalls, each one brimming with goods. The fresh vegetables all laid out would have you fooled it wasn't a Harvest festival display. The deep, shaded orange carrots dusted with mud, with the roots still attached. To eat these raw dipped into some hummus smothered in olive oil. To hear the loudness of the crunch is to experience the freshness. Then you find yourself sauntering over towards the Avenue des Trente. To you and I, bread heaven. Freshly baked seeded sourdough, bagels. focaccia, soda bread, naan, pitta, tortilla, pretzels, should I continue? Challah, ciabatta, rye and of course the baguette. Nothing beats a bit of stick and salted butter with some strawberry jam.

Oh, the French market is just incredible. I must book the ferry for next month, maybe I could take Finn, we could have a light lunch in the market square and have a mooch around the stalls.

Now before I get even more distracted, I need to find my keys, as I need to get myself to the office. The sooner, I get there the sooner I can get back home and who noes maybe see Finn. Scrambling through my wardrobe, I found a loose-fitting shirt, and a pair of beige pleated front trousers. I added a vintage, silk scarf I had not long owned having won it online after a bidding war. I then slid on some very old classic, Chanel ballet pumps and grabbed my work tote, along with my laptop and files.

Today was a roof down kind of day, to drive down the lanes in Jersey, with the roof down and the sea breeze washing over you was everything and more. Getting in my car, I couldn't help but smile at everything around me. I was so lucky to call this place my home, I will forever be in a debt to this island, I simply could never pay back the amount of joy it instilled within my heart.

Chapter Eleven

'Hey Bobby', smiled Jean.

'Hi Jean, did you get the Dropbox I sent you this morning?'

'Yes, thank you, I printed it and popped the letters in the post box about half an hour ago. Do you think you might have the Rigby case notes ready by the end of the week?'

'Absolutely, I plan on finishing the notes today. I will email everything over to you. If you need any amendments just let me know. How did Emma get on with that case yesterday in court?'

'Five years', she shook her head in dismay.

'Oh my, I think she was hoping for a better result than that.'

'I agree, but it was Judge Francis on duty', she added.

'Well, that explains that', I pointed my finger whilst rolling my eyes.

'There's some fresh coffee, and Johnathen brought Almond croissants in this morning, help yourself dear,' she smiled.

'

'Thanks Jean. I'm away on the course next week, could you let me know my flight times and forward my accommodation emails when you have a moment?'

'Yes, I will go do that now, before I forget and just so you know, the hotel includes evening meals and breakfast, so you need not look up restaurants and worry where to eat.'

'Jean you are a superstar,' I smiled.

'Keep an eye on your inbox,' she called whilst walking down the corridor.

Evening meals included I couldn't help but smile to myself. I find a huge proportion of my wages goes towards food. Why is it so blooming expensive. Only last week, I did what I call a 'top up' grocery shop. When I tell you I brought, a pizza, some sourdough, a bag of apples, a hand of bananas, a pack of chicken breasts and a bag of mixed leaf salad it was thirty-two pounds. That didn't even include a carton of Jersey milk which I buy from the local farm shop. Food is just so overly priced. So, excuse me if I celebrate that I have food included in my work trip for one whole week.

I didn't mind going into the office, it was in all fairness a very chilled environment considering we were immersed in a legal word. I even shared an office with Zoe which made things better. My desk was small, but when Zoe was not in the office, I used her desk, which allowed for me to spread my documents, bag and laptop on the surface. I checked the filing cabinet in case there was any extra work that needed doing but luckily for me, it was empty. Turning on my laptop and blowing gently over the steaming coffee which I had just got from the staff room, on route to the office. I was totally tempted to take a croissant, but I was strong and didn't cave into my sweet tooth. Now I was dating, I needed to look my best. Period.

Turning on my laptop, and opening the music app on my phone, I switched on my summer playlist and began to work on my to do list. Music in my ears, just made everything so much better, it allowed for time to pass and made my tasks just so pleasant.

I sat comfortably and allowed the next few hours to sail by without distraction. I wanted everything ticked off and that's exactly what I set out to do – just that!

Chapter Twelve

'Agnes', I called and waved frantically as I drove down the hill and headed back home. I pulled up on the side of road and wound down my window.

'Fancy seeing you, how are you today?' I asked.

'I'm good, I like to take a stroll down the street, change of scenery, gets a bit boring inside those four walls.'

'I've been to work, into the office, needed to get some work done without distractions and fancied a change too.'

'It's so warm today, we have such good weather forecast this week'.

'Glorious isn't it, do you have any plans today, Agnes?'

'Plans me?' She shook her head.

'Why don't you hop in and come to my cottage this afternoon until you get tired and have enough? I can drop you back home then if you like?'

'Bobby I would be delighted to see your cottage', she smiled.

'

'Do you need to bring anything with you? Bag? Medication?'

'No, I'm ready to hop into that lovely little vehicle of yours.'

'Come on then let's go', I smiled whilst reaching over the passenger seat to unlock the door.

'Have you been busy today?' Agnes asked whilst making herself comfy and buckling into her seat.

'Nothing crazy, I went into the office did a little bit of work there. Like you, it's nice to have a change of scenery.'

'Here, here', she blushed.

'Anything else to report? A young lady like you must have a pretty active social life.'

'Not as busy as you might think. Which when you come to think of it sounds diabolical. I think I'm what the world calls slightly introverted.'

'You will need to tell me the meaning of that word. I have little knowledge of how you, genzie's speak and the words you use.'

'Agnes check you out- genzie! Someone has been educating you,' I howled with disbelief.

'Heard it on that love programme, you know the dating one?'

'

'I do know of it yes, and you watch that?'

'Absolutely', she nodded.

I couldn't help but laugh, it was a little much to imagine Agnes watching a dating programme aimed at under thirties, but I take my hat off to her, she hasn't lost that youthful element to her personality.

'Well, an introvert, is someone who likes their own company, that's a quick way of answering your question and explaining it.'

'Word and a definition for everything nowadays. Utter rubbish. If it's not in the dictionary, then it's a load of tosh'.

'Well, let's not worry our heads on vocabulary. Fancy a coffee?'

'We're never here', she demanded.

'Yes, this is what I call home.'

'Oh, my goodness, Bobby, what a delightful little cottage you have. The garden, oh the garden, look at your roses. I must smell them'.

I walked around the car to help Agnes out. In all fairness she was strong on her legs but lacked confidence.

'I love roses, my favourite flower.'

'Mine too', she looked directly into my eyes, before strolling over to my flower bed which consisted mainly of roses and salvia and the odd allium.

'Beautiful, is this an Olivia?'

'Yes, I also have a Queen of Sweden to your left.'

'I had spotted that. These need some amphid control on them, you have terrible white fly.'

'I will see to that', I nodded.

'You must, they will suck the goodness out of the bud, you are very sheltered up here. That sea breeze is heavenly.'

'I know, comes in useful on a day like this. Take a seat Agnes, I'll go fetch some coffee. I happen to have sponge cake in the fridge. Would you like a slice?'

'Silly question Bobby', she hunched her shoulders and beamed.

'Be right back'.

I was delighted to have Agnes in my garden. I had developed such a warming to this kind, gentle, old lady. I loved her wicked sense of humour and expressions when she talked. I also liked being put in my place at times, I completely agree with her my roses needed attention, although between you and I, I had been blitzing them with water and washing up liquid, but the pesky flies won't budge. You would think I was mad if I told you I had wandered around my garden in search for ladybirds to put on the stems. I didn't feel it right though to tell her I had tried, it would have felt as though I was being rude. I had a complete respect for Agnes, a traditional respect of treating your elders in the correct manner. I fixed a tray with some coffee and my best cups and saucers. The Christmas mugs defiantly wouldn't do here. I added two slices of fresh sponge and some napkins and made my way back outside.

'You have a beautiful home. A home like this needs to be filled with a family, what are you plans for a family?'

'Oh', I paused slightly taken back.

'One day, maybe, but not yet, maybe in like ten years time.'

'That long! Career girl? You can juggle both you know'.

'Yeah, that's true, but I'm not ready yet. I want to travel and see the world, before I think or even explore that avenue.'

'You must follow your heart and dreams'.

'I think so too. I have a bucket list of places I want to see and things I want to do. I don't mean to be selfish, but I want to fulfil everything as an induvial before I open my life to anyone else,' I contemplated.

'Well, you need to do just that. You are not selfish Bobby; you would be a fool not to have fun in your years. So, I noticed there is no ring on your finger, why is that? A beautiful lady like you surely you have them queuing up.'

'No ring no, it's out there somewhere sitting in some jewellery shop, waiting for Mr right to buy it.'

'So, who are you courting?'

'Courting? What's that?' I questioned whilst downing a mouthful of sponge, because these questions were coming hard and fast.

'Courting as in dating, keep up dear', she said whilst adding some sugar to her coffee.

'I have met someone recently, he's called Finn.'

'Tell me more, does he have a perky bottom?'

'Oh, I can confirm he does indeed have a perky bottom', we both burst into laughter, yet another question I was not expecting.

'Jersey boy?'

'No, he's not long been here actually, he's from Ireland.'

'Irish, mmm, cheeky chappy's those Irishmen', she warned me.

'Finn is a surfing instructor; he comes from an equestrian background. He has the most wonderful, infectious personality,' I paused whilst thinking about our date.'

'Carry on', Agnes butted in.

'When I'm around him, I feel special. He is kind, funny and very romantic.'

'Sounds a catch'.

'I think he is. I go quite giddy when he talks so fast. I think it's his accent, it's so raw and deep.'

'So, he's the one then'.

'I think its way too early for me to make that assumption.'

'Well, you must have a feeling inside, don't waste your time if it feels like it's going nowhere. No one wants to be treated like a doormat.'

'Oh, it's not like that, I see every potential in Finn, he's got it all, looks, charm, personality. Plus, he's seriously fit.'

'Oh, he works out?'

'Well yes, but when I say fit, it kind of means handsome in your terminology.'

'I know what fit means Bobby, what your saying is, he is a bit of hot totty.'

'Just that', I laughed and squirmed at the same time. I didn't know how I felt about Agnes talking in such a way I would be talking to Zoe like. It was odd and weird, but the conversation made me laugh and I could tell from the look on her face she loved every moment.

'Did you date after you lost your husband Agnes?'

'No darling, even if I had wanted to, there would never be another man like my husband. I know he is with me every day, he lives here, in my heart', she touched her chest and smiled.

'That's beautiful. I think you were lucky to find someone who meant so much to you.'

'You will have the same, with Finn. I get a good feeling about this gentleman. I should meet him, give him the approval and once over.'

'Ha, I'm sure that could happen, erm be arranged,' I paused and slightly chocked on my own laughter.

'I will tell you a straight yes or no', she added.

'A yes, or no?' I questioned.

'

'Yes, I will give you my personal opinion if the relationship has potential.'

'Sounds good', I nodded.

I looked out towards the sea, in a slight disbelief that my relationship with my sexy Irishman was about to be judged by Agnes, and if it couldn't get even more nuts, I had completely agreed to it. My afternoon I had planned, had turned into a lecture and a form of relationship counselling all in one. I was enjoying every moment, but I also appreciated Agnes' words of wisdom, she had a whit, but she also told you how things were or were meant to be. I found Agnes, like a grandma I had never had.

'I need to get back for Crosslink, I never miss an episode.'

'What time is that on?'

'In about an hour', she said.

'Why don't I show you inside the cottage and around the rest of the garden.'

'That would be gold Bobby'.

'Come on then, follow me'.

I spent the next half an hour showing Agnes the inside of my cottage. You have probably guessed she had quite a lot to say about my décor and taste. I also, got a slight telling off about the dust she had found on my photo frames, but we will just skip past that part. Note to oneself, invest in a new feather duster, one that traps dust as opposed to swishing it around, so it deposits elsewhere. I had found though my tastes were quite similar to Agnes' which was a warming touch and allowed our conversation to flow, as we moved around the rooms.

'I best get you home, your carriage awaits Agnes', I smiled.

'Oh, I've had my Cinderella moment Bobby, you need to lose you're glass slipper and hope Finn surfaces at the right time to slip it on.'

'What do you mean?'

'Time will tell, a relationship only proves it's worth when its tested.'

'Meaning?'

'You will know what I mean when the moment happens. Trust this and be guided by this,' she held out her hand and placed it on my heart.

'Thanks Agnes'.

'Anytime, now do you want me to give you some rose spray for those pesky amphids. I can't bare the sight of those when I next visit. I have some in the shed, remind me when we get back to mine'.

'Sure, thing Agnes', I said bewildered. Evidently those aphids had really caused her an issue.

So, the remainder of the afternoon, involved me transporting Agnes back home; to have a tour of her garden and learn just about every technique and method I needed to control my aphid infestation. I felt such a need to race home and begin attacking these pesky little critters. I also felt the urgency to have them gone before she next visited and who knows let's face it, that visit could be quicker than we think. It amazed me the, I hate to use the word control more like the obedience I felt from Agnes. It was as though she was my grandma, and I was doing as I was told. That's how it felt. So much so, when I did return home, which was after also watching Crosslink sat next to Agnes, I did just that, attack the amphids. With my gardening gloves on, apron and rose clearing solution in hand, I went in to deal with the whitefly.

I also dropped Finn a sneaky text, which was of course, flirtatious and fun. Finn was having a quiet day of surfing lessons, so we were able to speak throughout the day. My stomach was brimmed full of butterflies doing loops like a track on an endless record. I felt excitement and was looking forward to seeing Finn again.

My afternoon of gardening, checking and responding to emails, whilst doing a little online retail therapy

'

collapsed into early evening and I found myself meeting Zoe and Kyle for a drink along with my friends down at Murphy's, in St Helier.

St. Helier was such a quaint town, busy in the day and quieter in the evenings. The once fishing village back in the 13th century, was the capital if you will of the island, it is not only home to Elizabeth Castle but also is the chair for the islands government and where you will find most the shops and businesses. I always found the town shimmering in glamour, to walk up and down the beautiful stretch of King Street with a Voisin's or DeGruchy carrier was something to boast about or as us genzis would say 'goals'.

Chapter Thirteen

'Surprise!' cheered an Irish accent as I opened the front door.

'Finn!' I gasped.

'I brought some beers and popcorn', he smirked.

'I text you all of five minutes ago and you proclaimed to have been in the bath'.

'Yeah, it was a quick five-minute bath and proclaimed? Someone has had their head in a classic book'.

'Oh, I can see it was quick -you, bathed, texted me and got dry and dressed and drove to mine all in 4 minutes since you sent that very text informing me you were in the bath. As for the book, of course classics- can't beat being a timeless romantic'.

'So now that's been dealt with, fancy a beer?'

I couldn't help but smile at his gorgeous face, and in all fairness any woman would be happy to see a well fit, Irishman at her front door, but I'll be honest with you I was frustrated to hell at the sight of him seeing me in such a state. When I tell you I was wearing an overworn, vintage band hoody and a pair of denim hotpants, complete with a huge, fizzy pineapple hair bun and sporting zero makeup, you get my drift here. I didn't want Finn seeing me looking like such a toe.

'You look cute', he smiled.

'Cute, come on Finn, I hardly scream gf material look at the state of me'.

'I am looking', he smiled.

'And you agree with me, so yeah pass me a blooming beer'.

'Here you go and no, I don't agree, your perfect, exactly as you are.'

'Shut up!'

'No, I won't be told to shut up Bobby. I can't get enough of you. I was lying when I told you I was in the bath because I wanted to surprise you. I want to spend my evening with you, especially as Corbin has told me you and Zoe are going back to the mainland.'

'Sorry, I was going to tell you about my work trip, I have only just had the details finalised today.'

'I know, I heard Zoe telling Corbin all about it. I'm going on a little trip myself. Corbin is sending me to Guernsey for the day and I'm catching the ferry back the following day. Need to pick up some gear from his dad's surf shop.'

'Cool, I've never been to Guernsey, I wish I was coming with you.'

'I know, would have been a romantic getaway'.

'I'm sure we will have plenty of them to look forward to, that's if you can bear the sight of me again.'

'Bobby, you're beautiful, besides that hoody is pretty epic.'

'Yup, it was my dad's it's like twenty years old.'

'Vintage'.

'Thank you.'

'For what bringing you a beer?'

'No, you idiot'.

'You don't say idiot like that, you say eejit.'

'You know that accent….'

'Oh yeah', he smiled whilst pulling me tightly into his arms.

'It sends my mind wild and into overdrive'.

'You send me wild Bobby'.

'Let's be wild together then', I whispered into his ears, before he carried me away into his arms. Let's say the rest of the evening became history.

Chapter Fourteen

'I hate packing, its such a chore', moaned Zoe.

'You should get some of those packing cubes they are magic for packing.'

'I wish you was coming'.

'I never thought to check my passport, I just presumed it was in date.'

'Easy mistake Bobby don't beat yourself up. I will miss you though. I was hoping to do some retail therapy with my bestie.'

'Well, I've probably saved myself from going into a small debt there. You are a bad influence when it comes to shopping.'

'You could have gone with Finn though to Guernsey, sure they haven't had a cancellation on the ferry?' asked Zoe.

'I keep refreshing the page but sadly nothing.'

'At least the weather is good'.

'Yeah true, I was looking forward to it though.'

'

'I'll facetime you. Right, that's me done, time to call a cab and get to the airport.'

'You sure you don't want me to give you a lift.'

'No, I want you to keep checking the ferry website in case a ticket comes available.'

'Okay'.

'I'll leave my spare keys under the wellington boot plant pot'.

'Got it'.

'Okay, catch you later.'

'Bye hun, safe travels.'

So yeah, me being the stupid fool I am, I completely forgot that my passport was out of date. I felt awful calling into work to explain, I looked like such a lemon, and I felt totally unprofessional. I guess, it had just slipped my mind, but my excuse and reasoning were valid enough. Since moving to Jersey, I had no need to go on holiday. The scenery, the beaches, the weather, I had no reason to leave this beautiful island that had wrapped itself around my heart.

I decided to treat myself today as I was told, I had no need to go into work, so fancied a walk along Gorey beach or long beach as the locals call it. Gorey beach was snuggled into the Royal Bay of Grouville. I personally found Gorey village one of the quaintest and laid-back parts of Jersey. To me time felt as though it had stood still. The atmosphere felt very French to me with its delicately painted pastel buildings which were mainly restaurants or cafes and beautiful old school hotel. The bay stood in all its glory with the crown being Mont Orgueil Castle, a queen in her own right, to have a tour of this compelling piece of history was nothing short of an escapism.

Sounds ridiculous but the first time I visited the castle, I felt like a princess, looking down on her land. The excitement of moving to live in Jersey was all a little much and every stone, landmark and now castle to me felt like treasure. To stand in the castle walls and look below you and see the little fishing boats bobbing on the gentle waters, coupled with the view of locals socialising and making small talk in the village over a coffee, filled me with hope. Believe me when I tell you, I'm very much a modern girl with every piece of technology on the market, but there is something about being here on this island, which removes you from that modern world. People actually talk, they don't just text or call, people stand for periods of time actually just talking – remember when we were kids and the mall (shopping centre) would be crammed at Christmas time, people laughing, talking absorbing the day to its fullest not a mobile phone in sight. Whereas now you find everyone glued to their screens, clutching their device as though it's oxygen, vital and necessary to function. It's sad really, when you think of how we live today. Yet, here in Jersey, I feel a million miles away from the modern world, time has stood still here. I hope the island never looses that feeling of nostalgia and warmth. The people here or islanders as they prefer to be called are so pure, honest and happy.

The ride to Gorey was always a breeze, and the parking always effortless. I was glad to be stood at the tip of the beach, inhaling the richness of the sea air.

'Bobby how's it going?' I heard a voice from behind.

'Jacob', I cheered in delight.

'What you up to? Time for a coffee?' he enquired.

'You know what coffee sounds great; might you squeeze to a cinnamon roll?'

'Seeing as it's you Bobsta'.

Jacob hooked his arm around my elbow, and we strolled down the path towards the Italian bistro. Jacob was one cool dude; we had such a good friendship. I just want to clarify – that's what our relationship was a friendship of the purest form. Despite people saying we were close (aka Kyle) there was no flirtatious or romantic desire between us. We weren't attracted to each other, we just bounced off each other's personalities.

'What can I get you?' asked the waitress.

'Two cappuccino's and two pastries please', blurted Jacob.

'Chocolate sprinkles on top?' she continued to ask.

'Hell yeah', he beamed.

'If you have a flake, you could always add one of those too', I added.

The waitress walked off giggling to herself and I just smiled smugly.

'She was checking you out', I boasted.

'You reckon?' he asked.

'Totes babe, haven't you heard I'm a spoken for woman now', I questioned.

'You know I've already heard, you were the one that was chewing off my ear the other night at 3 am'.

'Oh yeah, sorry about that, I couldn't sleep, and I noticed you were online, why was you awake?'

'Didn't get in till two, then I put the tv on and time just slipped by. That's the problem working in a pub- you become nocturnal'.

'Delightful. Well, I should be on a works trip, but it fell through last minute, so got the day off, well afternoon considering I had a slow morning at home.'

'You happy?' he questioned further.

'You know what Jacob, I haven't felt so happy inside in such a long time. You need to meet Finn, you will like him, he even paid your craftsmanship a compliment'.

'Considering I had never panelled a wall; I did do a sick job'.

'Oh, I love it, so much so, I was thinking about refreshing the kitchen, nothing heavy, just a lick of paint and some new handles.'

'I can help you with that, pick up some paint samples and I will come over and help you choose.'

'Oh great.'

'I've applied for a new job, well, a promotion at Murphys. Amanda is leaving so I've applied for her position'.

'You will totally get it, you must. There is no way they will lose you or hire a new person. You're the beating heart of Murphys.'.

'I love that place. I would love to own a pub like Murphys.'

'You will'.

'If you say so, is this the whole power of manifestation?'

'Absolutely, it's a thing trust me. I look how much my life has changed and I think back to how life was on the mainland. I'm living proof positivity and manifestation works.'

'You are living the Jersey dream'.

'I truly am. I'm so lucky to be here Jacob. I love Jersey its just everything and more,' I teared up.

'Oh Bobsta', he got up and hugged me.

'Bobby?' said a random voice which wasn't Jacob's but sounded familiar.

'Corbin…' I stuttered.

'You good', he said whilst giving me a high five.

'Yeah good, just catching up with a friend', I added.

'I can see, did Finn get to Guernsey okay? Hasn't text me yet.'

'Yeah, we spoke earlier, he didn't stay on the phone for long he felt sick from the crossing', I said whilst unwrapping Jacob's arm from around me.

'So, are you going to introduce me to your friend?' he gloated in a tone that didn't suit his persona I had come to associate with him.

'Corbin this is Jacob, he works at Murphys in town. Jacob is one of my closest friends here.'

'Good to meet you Jacob, I run the surf shack at St Ouen, so if you fancy a board, hit me up.'

'No, I don't do the water mate, not my thing, I'm more of a pint and pack of crisps guy, watching the footie on the big screen', said Jacob in a low blow tone.

'Cool, each to their own, well, I will catch you around Bobby, you look lovely today,' smiled Corbin before turning to walk away.

I could tell from Jacob's eyes he was not remotely impressed by Corbin. I sensed an atmosphere between all three of us. It was awkward and uncomfortable.

'That's Zoe's bf'.

'No, just no', he shook his head and rested the palms of his hands over his sage green eyes.

'Yup, you know, he was kind of off with me then. Normally he is really outgoing and full of …'

'Himself', burst out Jacob.

'Shhh… well yes but he was quite rude then. I didn't like that streak he showed.'

'Maybe he's having a bad day. I don't think I would hold it to him. Zoe seems happy, she's had it rough too when it comes to men, I think you should just let it pass.'

'Yeah, you are probably right, bad day, we all get them'.

I don't know what it was. I chose to agree with Jacob to his face, but I knew inside something was just off. Deeply off, I always go by gut instinct and its usually right, unless it's my gut instinct on the weather, that I always get wrong.

'I need to love you and leave you honeybun', said Jacob.

'Don't you have time for a refill?' I questioned.

'No, I need to go pick up a suit for a wedding before work. We should meet up later this week and I'll help you choose a paint colour for the kitchen.'

'That would be great, I'll order in a pizza, and we can swatch and eat at the same time.'

'Perfecto my sweet pea, now I need to leave, bye Bobby.'

'See you later', I smiled.

Chapter Fifteen

Walking along the beach, I contemplated on my coffee with Jacob, he was such a good guy. I valued the friendship I had with him. The bond had been structured on a solid foundation from the first time we met, which now seems like a lifetime ago. I was still pondering on Corbin's attitude too; it was just so off. That encounter with him didn't sit right with me. In reality I wanted to pick up my mobile and call Zoe, but I was hesitant because I knew she would defend him, it's what you do when your loved up in a new bubble and can't see beyond the heart chambers. I didn't want to implicate our friendship on just a feeling I had, even though I knew deep down he had shown a side of him, I didn't like, a nasty streak if you will.

Inhaling the sea air into my lungs felt so good from inside. With my feet on the sand, grounded to the earth, I felt rejuvenated from my head right through to my bones. There was something quite nostalgic about being on the shore, which brought my core back to my childhood and I felt the need every visit to look for quirky shells. The treasure of the sea, washed up on the sand waiting to be discovered. I had incorporated shells at home into my décor in the bathroom. They

'

were very fitting. I even had sewn shells onto some of my clothing, made jewellery and weaved them into my hair braids at times.

I kneeled to dust the damp sand from some of the tops of the shells. Brown, taupe, mauve, tan, coiled, curled and crumbled shells of all kinds rested upon the sand.

'Ow!' I squealed.

What felt like a sharp prick was indeed a piece of fractured glass. Rubbing away the seeping blood from the small cut which appeared to be like a waterfall protruding from my finger. I squeezed the area with a piece of tissue luckily, I was carrying in my pocket and rubbed away the sand to reveal a glass bottle containing a note.

This felt all so very much like a sailor fairytale moment, and a nostalgic character who loved to eat spinach and sported some impressive muscles came to mind, if you know you know. Pinching the note from the tight broken area of glass, I pulled out the note. I felt excited to find such washed up treasure. In my headspace I felt as though I had struck gold. A nugget of priceless worth.

My head was filled with questions, what if it's an SOS? Or a letter to a lover. A map of a treasure chest or a pirate island which no one knows about. Shaking my head and telling myself to act my age, I unravelled the note.

Standing here, on the cliff top of the bay, looking out across the land of my hometown, I see the beauty that nature has offered. The eternal gift of mother earth that never stops giving. These last few weeks I've seen the world in a different light. I guess they call it adulting. Instead of wanting to reach for my games console or go to the pub with the boys. I've needed more. I keep questioning myself if I'm okay and I'm not having a manic moment, but I feel the need to go on my own journey. Deep down, this voice keeps calling me from within, to go follow the path I want. I want to be by the ocean, work by the ocean, wake up by the ocean. I can't get the bloody sight of blue out of my mind. My grandpa once said to me 'May the dreams you hold dearest be those which come true.' My dream is to work and live by the ocean and find love. I want to find love and for it to be like a cosy Irish cottage, warm, inviting and filled with memories to last a lifetime.

It's written in the stars somewhere, I'm sure....

I hope I found the girl and end up living in the quaint cottage crammed with Irish charm, which rests beside the sea.

Maybe I'm pathetic, maybe I'm daft, but it's my calling. There must be some mischievous leprechaun out there who reads this and can point me in the right direction. Not the direction to the rainbow to find the pot of gold.

I don't want the pot of gold; I want the girl.

‘

Chapter Sixteen

A wave of sickness ran over my body with a hefty weight. The sickness was for sure not from the height of the cliffs, having now driven to Corbière. Upon finding that note, which instantly bailed me over. I felt the need to be in Corbiere. There was something about being here which allowed me to feel the air in my lungs. Each breath, clearing the cobwebs which had clung for dear life. To feel air so pure, was to fly through the blue skies without wings. Freedom on every level.

The crumbled rocky boulders which lay weathered and fixed, allowed for a vision out to sea like no other. The wind was always or at least felt so strong here. To hear the soundtrack of waves crashing against the rocks, dispersing their foamy froth across the surface of the waves, was a sound exploding in delight. It was also a sight which never bored me. I could easily get lost in a world of non-existence just sitting here. Corbiere or should I say La Corbiere is home to the first lighthouse in the British Isles built from concrete. There you go, they say you learn something new every day, so there is a nugget of information for the day. It's just so calming here, situated in the most south- western part of the island, I'm lucky this gem, is near to me.

'

However, I have got caught out once or twice with the tide timetable. Not the best experience of my life, I must admit, but I won't embarrass myself by filling you in on that story.

Despite feeling sick, from the contents of that letter, I managed to find a few coins at the bottom of my bag, enough at least for a cone of ice-cream. Don't judge ice-cream fixes everything.

Walking further towards the path of the lighthouse, I found a more sheltered spot to enjoy my extra creamy pot of yummy goodness. Jersey ice cream is just so delicious. I love a tub of chocolate fudge Sundae from that brand which we all love and pay extortionate for at the cinemas, but there's something about Jersey Ice -cream - it just hits different!

Looking down towards my pocket I could feel the note burning my skin with its existence. That note just had to be written by Finn. There was no way it couldn't have been. Reading the note, I felt this crushing of Finn's presence all around. The feeling of nausea sept over my body. I had an essence of guilt of overstepping something which evidently was so private. How could I look at Finn again, knowing I knew about his deep inner feelings, which even he by the sounds of it couldn't talk about to anyone, not even his family.

'

The enjoyable me time which I had hoped to have had, stopped abruptly and the sheer delight of Corbiere, had passed. I looked at Finn's letter once more, with a tear travelling down my cheek. I wanted to give him hug. I wanted to tell him I knew all about his feelings and I was somehow going to be that girl at the end of his rainbow. I had the cottage fuelled with charm which rested beside the sea (which is a little eerie that's what he'd wished for) nether the less, I had it.

If I told Finn, I found the letter, would he even believe me if I told him I had found it only today. I doubt that it would probably cross his mind, that I'd stubbled across the letter, and I set out to find an Irish guy who happens to be a surfer.

The whole thing, just stunk to the core, of a mangled web of what ifs. If only I had made sure my passport was all in order. This would never have happened, I would probably be in London with Zoe having a whale of a time and not caught in a fisherman's sea net of just utter polluted woes.

I hopped back in my car, and followed the windy cliff top roads, which sent my anxiety into overdrive. That was one part of jersey I loathed, the cliff top roads, which had no barriers of protection. It was just you, your car and a few inches of land, with a sheer drop down below, waiting like some sea monster to scoop you up.

Having managed to escape the sea monster, I drove towards home, whist briefly pulling over to the honesty box on the side of the road. This box was a treasure chest in its own right. Whoever owned and filled this box really did care about its contents for today, it was filled with homemade, sticky jams, lavender honey and sponge cakes. I wasn't here for any of that though, I sifted through the few bunches of cut flowers and chose two bunches of freshly cut peonies. Leaving a ten-pound note in the money box, I continued my journey and headed towards Agnes'.

Swinging my car into her rather large driveway, I rang the bell but there was no answer. Looking through the windows, I couldn't see Agnes, and her television was turned off. Presuming she was out, I opened her porch which was unlocked and left a bunch of pastel pink, peonies resting upon her door, with a message to say they were from me. I knew they would brighten her day. There is something about having flowers in the home, that just makes you smile each time you walk past them. I always think when your gifted flowers or you buy them for yourself (which you should always do ladies), they are a gift from nature which simply keeps on giving.

Chapter Seventeen

Hopping in the warm, inviting shower and allowing the steam to purify my skin, was nothing short of pure bliss. Inhaling the essential oils from my shower scrub was beyond relaxing. The ylang ylang wafts of heaven, were divine. I could have stood under the shower head for much longer than I normally care to be in the shower for. At heart I was a bath girly. It felt so good to feel the water running through my hair. The need to feel clean was such a craving. If I could have washed my mind of that note, then to be frank I would have. I felt like I was keeping some dirty secret, that I had betrayed Finn. At heart I know that wasn't the case, but telling myself it was mind in overdrive just didn't cut it.

Stepping out the shower, I wrapped a warm towel around me from the heated rail. A warm towel was such a treat, a warm fuzzy embrace to greet you when you dither as you get out the shower. Throwing my hair into a towel turban, I headed towards the kitchen to pour myself a glass of something sparkly. Don't

'

judge me, I'm not a day drinker, but I made an exception for today.

'Bobby', I heard the door knock and someone call my name.

Why at this moment does someone need to be knocking my door. Maybe I should leave it, whoever it is will go away. I could just about make out a shadow through the glass pane which framed the oak door. I crept along the hallway and silently up the stairs to catch a glimpse of who it was. Peering through the window in the spare bedroom which I happened to use as a dressing room, come storage room, come dumping ground if you will. I could make out a masculine body.

'Oh shoot', I uttered.

I shuddered at the sight of Corbin. There was no way I was going to answer the door to that rude, obnoxious pig. After my meeting with him earlier, I certainly didn't want to give him any of my time. My thoughts on him had completely shifted. I hadn't even thought on how to raise my concerns with Zoe. How would she believe me, she was smitten with Corbin, the way I was smitten with my Finn.

Spying on his every move, I managed to work out through the light shadow against the wall he had walked away form my front door. Thank heavens, I was safe and had swerved that encounter. Balancing 'my turban hair bun, whilst walking running down the stairs, I made a bee line for that glass of wine, which now I was gasping for.

'Aghhh !!!' I screamed at the top of my lungs.

'I did knock, evidently you were showering so didn't hear me', smirked Corbin.

'Yeah, I was in the shower', I added.

'You should have left that glass of wine in the fridge and poured it after the shower, quite warm in here. Quite a sun trap you have on the back garden', he wailed, which sent shudders down my spine.

'I was already out the shower; I just ran back upstairs to fetch my slippers.'

'Where are they?' he questioned.

'Where are what?'

'Your slippers, your bare foot', he noted.

'Couldn't find them, my crocs will do', I replied whilst sliding my feet into my beige crocs.

'You going to pour me a glass?'

'Sure, sorry I should have asked, would you like red or white?'

'Red', he replied.

'

As I poured the glass of wine, my heart and mind were pacing speeds of ridicule. Even the palms of my hands were sweaty.

'Here, you go'.

'Cheers to finding the one'.

'Finding the one?' I nearly spat my drink out.

'Yeah, I found Zoe, you found Finn, life's magic'.

'To finding the one', I clinked my glass against his, whilst feeling rather awkward dressed in just a towel.

'Relax Bobby', he said whilst rubbing his hand over my naked shoulder.

'What can I do for you?' I enquired.

'I was thinking about taking Zoe away for a weekend, just wanted to ask you for some pointers.'

'You're the one dating her, I'm sure you know what pointers to add.'

'Feisty and hot, two credentials I like in a woman'.

'Is that all?' I said.

'Have I offended you, Bobby? I'm only paying you a compliment.'

'No, you haven't offended me, I just don't think it's your place to call me hot. I'm dating Finn, your friend.'

'My employee', he said smugly in a cool tone.

'Employee, friend whatever… I'm with Finn and I'd prefer it if you left. If you want to surprise Zoe, then I suggest you do it off your own back.'

'You are so sexy when you're angry, did anyone ever tell you that?'

'Yeah, you!'

'I'm sensing a bit of hostility towards me Bobby. What you need to remember is that I'm not the one going for coffee, if that's what you call it with other men.'

'What are you talking about other men?' I raised my voice.

'This morning slipped your mind', he noted.

'You're talking about Jacob? Oh my days, he's a friend, a good friend.'

'If that's what you call it', he moved closer back towards me, before resting his glass on the side unit.

'That's all it is', I pleaded.

'I don't blame you, although maybe you can't help it. You know when I first saw you and Zoe, I remember 'walking towards you and thinking how beautiful you were.'

'You mean Zoe', I took a step backwards, as Corbin felt a little close for comfort.

'Zoe wasn't even in my vision. You, looked so beautiful, your hair blowing in the wind looking across the bay.'

'I think you should go', I said whilst turning my back and walking away.

'Bobby wait'.

Corbin pulled my arm with enough force which spun me round and into his arms, in a demi embrace. With his hands placed around my waist, he pulled my towel towards him. My heart was pounding through my rib cage, each thud louder than the previous. Before I knew it Corbin's lips were touching mine, to my horror.

'Get off me! Leave now. How dare you try to kiss me! I wouldn't look at you, if you were the last man on this planet.'

'Bobby, calm down,' he reached his arm out towards my shoulders.

'I said GO !'

'

'Fine, but we both know you kissed me back, you didn't pull away straight away'.

'What are you talking about, you had me locked into you against the kitchen worktop. I couldn't move'.

'Course Bobby. I'll be waiting when Finn finishes with you.'

'Finishes with me', I shouted.

'He will not look at you again, two men in one day. Coffee with the bestie and afternoon fumbles with his boss. We both know you want me and not Finn'.

'You're mad'.

'Only mad for you Bobby, why can't you just see that, come on, I can give you everything you want. I have my own business, house, sportscar…' he walked back towards me.

'OUT NOW!' I screamed at the top of my lungs.

Corbin walked out the back door on my order. I slid down the cabinet and onto the floor in a crumpled heap, bursting into tears. I had never felt so humiliated and disgusted at the same time. How dare he kiss me, then say I kissed him back. I felt so bad and hurt inside. I had betrayed my best friend and boyfriend in the space of thirty minutes.

'Bobby, are you okay dear?'

'Agnes? What are you doing in my house, how long have you been here for?'

'I took a stroll this morning and caught the bus to your cottage. You were out, so I checked the plant pot for a key.'

'And you let yourself in? That's very funny Agnes; you must be thirsty can I get you a drink?'

'No, I have one, I made myself useful and dead headed those roses of yours. I took some of the over ripe lemons from your tree and made some lemonade. Would you like a glass? I have plenty in the lounge. I must have drifted off asleep in there, waiting for you.'

'Lemonade sounds perfect,' I smiled with an eternal gratitude, that Agnes was here. I didn't care that she had let herself in, that's Agnes' personality all over cheeky and spontaneous. If anything, I was so happy to see her, I needed her comforting presence.

'Don't cry dear', she tapped my hand.

'Arrogant pig', she scowled.

'Tell me about it, that's Zoe's boyfriend.'

'I know dear, I was watching and listening to everything.'

'You were? I never cheated on Finn. Corbin threw himself onto me'.

'You are lucky to be having men lunging themselves at you. I wish I were forty years or so younger,' she giggled which sent us both into hysterics.

'Today has been a nightmare,' I huffed.

'We all have days like that, everyday can't be perfect Bobby.'

'I guess so'.

'Why don't you go fix a robe around you and comb your hair through, I'll fix us some biscuits from your kitchen and you can tell me all about it,' smiled Agnes' with her eyes sparkling back at me.

'Thank you Agnes'.

'What for?'

'For being my friend', I said gently.

Chapter Eighteen

'So, you see, I was only walking along the beach, I never set out to cut myself and find the letter', I added.

'It's just a letter Bobby, and if you ask me it found its rightful recipient', said Agnes.

'I feel as though I know things that I shouldn't know, that it will always be there in my mind and somehow I will be making the contents of that letter come true.'

'That's good though, because he would have found his match.'

'Wouldn't it all be a little fabricated?' I questioned.

'No because, that saying about the cottage being like a cosy Irish home. It's a true saying in Ireland. You couldn't have made that up, nor could you have made up the fact you live in a cottage too. This is the part where I should probably mention my husband was Irish too, but born here on the island.'

'Did he have an accent?'

'Oh yes, his mother had a very strong dialect. With marrying him, my home became very much full of Irish charm and warmth. Not to mention tradition. My husband even had a Guinness barrel to pour draft from 'in the dining room. Take a look when you next come over.'

'That so sweet.'

'Bobby when you fall in love with an Irishman, its somehow different. They have this mannerism, this way of capturing you with their relaxed chit chat of utter nonsense which somehow takes the weight off your feet and makes you feel light. Your glass will always be full, never half measured. When I say full, yes with a Guiness or a measure of whisky, but also full of joy and happiness. A happy heart Bobby. With an Irishman you will not only have his love but his commitment to you and his future children. He will create a family; he holds with his strong hands of protection. When your babies eventually leave home, and you think about all the years you've danced through so quickly yet so smoothly, you're Irishman will be the one who will waltz you around the kitchen by candlelight. Just the two of you. Holding you tightly, he will look you in the eye, with the same look he gave you when he first cast eyes on you, when you agreed to marry him and when he saw you in wedding dress walking down the aisle. You're Irishman, you're Finn will have rescued you, just like you would have rescued him,' said Agnes slowly.

'That was beautiful', I sobbed.

'That's your life Bobby- beautiful.'

'What about Corbin?' I said.

'Sorry whose Corbin?'

'The guy who was here just.'

'Oh him, so insignificant I had forgot about that schmuck.'

'Agnes !'

'I hadn't forgot about him, I knew who he is. My point is forget about him, he's irrelevant. Let him mouth off, have his moment. There will be some blonde flick her hair and he will soon swoon in.'

'What about Zoe?'

'I think you should be honest with your friend, and air your worries. If she chooses to go cold on you, then let that be. The heat will fizzle soon enough, and your friendship will stand forward.'

'You're better than any encyclopaedia', I added.

'I've been called a few choice words in my life but never an encyclopaedia.'

'Well, you should be delighted to have such a reference. You have filled me with hope Agnes.'

'I was once a young lady like you. It's all down to life experiences.'

'Thank you Agnes.'

'No need to thank me, what are friends for,' she smiled.

Agnes was such a charming lady, fuelled with a wealth of experience and knowledge. I felt better having now calmed down and talked the events of the day through with Agnes.

'Can I give you a ride home, crossthingy..majiggy starts soon on tv.'

'You remembered my programme on television, how kind. What with your memory and my words of wisdom we make a fine team.'

'We do Agnes, we really do'.

Chapter Nineteen

Slipping my feet into my fluffy slippers, I eventually sat down for the evening. Some time had passed since I had dropped Agnes home. Having been overwhelmed with her peonies on her arrival back home, she invited me in for a cup of tea, which then turned into me cooking us both a bacon sandwich. Mine of course had lashings of ketchup, whereas Agnes hit the brown sauce hard. I thought I had too much sauce on my sandwich, well her measure I can confirm was nothing short of pure greed. Washed down with yet more tea, and a bowl of sticky toffee pudding and custard, I had quite the food baby growing from my stomach.

Today's events had most definitely been rescued by Agnes by her super power cape of wisdom. I never dreamt I would form such a bond with a lady of her age. When I say that I don't mean old. I mean I didn't expect to have similar interest and hold such conversations with her. Sometimes when I spoke with Agnes' it was as though I was stuffed under the duvet having a sleep over with Zoe. Behind Agnes' frail exterior and tired, aged skin, shone a lady, with a heart of pure gold, no goldsmith could put a value on.

I was glad to be winding down the evening. The moonlight shone against the water, illuminating St

Brelade's with its delicate light. Taking a brief wonder into the garden and smelling the damp, cool air, felt refreshing against my partially sunburnt skin. With all the commotion of the day, I hadn't applied any sunscreen, so was sporting a lobster look on my shoulders and the tip of my nose. A huge red blob of red at the end of my nose which I had plastered in after sun, would have given Rudloph nose envy for sure. With that thought casting a shadow over my mind, I felt my phone vibrating in my pocket.

'Hey Finn', I smiled.

'My girl, how are you?'

'Missing you'.

'I miss you too, but I'll be back soon enough. I didn't want to go to sleep without hearing your voice,' he whispered.

'I'm glad you called.'

'Texting doesn't cut it'.

'Not when I can hear that accent', I smiled to myself.

'How do you fancy dinner at that fancy restaurant in St Aubin when I get back?'

'I heard the lobster is incredible there'.

'Well, we best find out for ourselves. I'll book us a table.'

'Finn….'

'Yeah'

There was a silence on the call which felt like a never-ending pause. I wanted to tell him everything.

'Sorry…' I hesitated. 'I'm just tired forgive me.'

'Bobby, I want you to know, meeting you has made me so happy. I want you… I want us.'

'Oh Finn', I bit my lip allowing a tear to shed from the corner of eye.

'Night angel'.

'Goodnight Finn'.

'

Chapter Twenty

Allowing the next few days to fold before my eyes, I managed to bi-pass Finn like the plague. Believe me when I tell you I wanted to feel his touch against my skin, hear his voice in person and be romanced by candlelight. However, call me what you will I was a jelly belly. The only promising thing at the moment was Zoe had decided to extend her stay on the mainland. We of course had made idle chit chat, amicably agreeing to just about everything she had to say. Corbin had even tried to call me, saying he had got my number from Finn's phone which had turned my stomach sideways.

Throwing my head into work had been a wonderful distraction. I was probably if anything working too hard for someone who had told their boss they had come down with sudden flu.

'Why are you hiding this is ridiculous, I'm highlighting you're hair in your house and using the kitchen sink as a wash basin', scorned Kyle.

'It was you who said my hair was desperate', I flipped back.

'Bobby you need to get yourself out of this relationship if this is what it's doing to you.'

'It's not the relationship, its just everything around it.'

'Just take the time out yeah, you don't need to be hiding in your house, faking flu, just throw the blooming note back in the sea in a new bottle and forget all about it.'

'You will keep it under your lid about the bottle?'

'Yes, but I'm glad you told me, there you go take a look in that filthy mirror of yours'.

'Don't you start on my dusting technique. It looks great, thank you'.

'You look great! Well, you will do when you change your clothes and swig a bottle of mouthwash. Bobby do what you need to do, put yourself first'.

'I will, how much do I owe you?'

'Nothing! Call it a free therapy session'.

'Kyle, I love you,' I smiled.

'I'm taken babes, Italian stallion lives in St Peter'.

'You can fill me in the details of that one later. I'm going to have a wash and get my life in order.'

'Later baby!' said Kyle while letting himself out the door. I did happen to feel fresh. Bending to throw my hear back and forth to give it my personal jush, my phone rang, and the fear of dread sank my stomach to the floor.

'Hey Finn', I croaked in a fake sore throat kind of voice.

'Come outside the front, I want to air kiss you'.

'Coming', I squealed from inside. This is not happening why is he here.

Opening the door and stepping out I was greeted by Finn blowing me kisses and in turn catching the ones I blew back.

'You had your hair done? It looks a lot lighter than last night on facetime.'

'Yeah, it was just a spare of the moment thing, I agreed to be Kyle's model, he was just messing around really. Besides my highlights needed a touch up,' I said whilst spinning a web of fabricated lies. I felt an instant sickness of the person I was becoming.

'You look great!'

'I need a hug', I hesitated.

'Me too, try not to give me the lurgy', he joked.

'I think I'm over it to be fair, I was just being over cautious'.

Hugging Finn was a warming comfort, pure and gentle. I loved this side of Finn. I was all for the cheeky Irish charm, but the sensitive side he often hid, was the side that melted the walls to my heart.

'I need to tell you something', I paused.

'What?'

'I erm… think we should go for dinner to that restaurant we had talked about'.

'I'll see if they can squeeze us in for this evening, you sure you are okay?' he squeezed my arm whilst checking my forehead temperature with the back of his hand.

'Perfect'.

'I'm going to go back to work; I'll text you about tonight.'

'Yeah, let me know the time, I'll meet you there.'

Finn walked away back towards his car. I knew in my mind and from the voice within, I needed to put an end to either Finn and I, or an end to the shenanigans of the last few days. I couldn't continue like this lying, being deceitful and faking being ill. It wasn't me. Looking over the fence down on to the bay, my heart couldn't help but smile at the beautiful sandy white beach, and icy pale waters. An ocean so blue, so big and strong had held Finn's secret bottled message. That's when I realised just that.

This note wasn't mine to keep. It had found its way to me by sheer chance. The point of a message in the bottle is for it to surface at some point and be read. That had happened. I knew what I needed to do, so I set on my mission, to take a stroll down to the bay.

Pulling on some shorts and a baggy t-shirt, I slid on some sandals and used the gate which revealed a steep path down to the bay. Not exactly ideal for flip flops, but needs must, and I knew at this hour a car parking space would be impossible.

Clenching the note in the palms of my hands along with a Kilner bottle I used normally for smoothies. I rested my legs momentarily on the sand, which burnt as it hit my toes. It was so warm today, the heat was muggy and sticky, not even the breeze was strong enough to cool you down. Taking off my sandals, I wiggled the sand in between my toes, stroked my fingers in the sand creating a heart with the letters B and F inside.

Taking pen to paper, I inhaled the biggest breath of salty goodness and opened my heart with an incision any cardiologist would boast about.

You found your way to me and washed-up surfing on the shore of St Ouen, the same way your letter did that day at Gorey. Since then, the last few days I felt a guilt and the truth is I have no reason to be guilty. But it's how I feel. I want to tell you so badly that I know you're wish. Then part of me says, from now on I would just be fabricating life according to your letter. Do I make sense?

Finn I'm so madly in love with you. I can't stop thinking about you, I've never been so happy in all my life. I want to spend the rest of my life with you in my cosy little cottage, besides the sea. A home with you filled with joy and if you're lucky maybe one day a Guinness draft tap (that surely counts towards the

'Irish cottage origin of living in a cosy Irish cottage).

I began a journey like yours when I moved to Jersey. I longed to be happy and find myself, which through making friends, starting a new job which threw me in the deep end at first and then doing my mini reno of the cottage, I did just that. Then somehow, you appeared and taught me about how to love and in return be loved.

I want to be with you Finn, love you a lifetime, nurture who knows even a family of our own. Marry you in the fisherman's chapel at St Brelade. That feels good to say that out loud. I've never told anyone that, but the first time I stepped foot in that church, I imagined and even walked myself down the aisle, pretending I was wearing a white dress, draped in lace and decorated with pearl accents.

I'm sorry if I ever broke your trust by finding your letter, I never intended to.

Say one day when I'm old and snuggled next to you drinking hot cocoa one Christmas Eve, I'll look back at this whole scenario and laugh about it and if we don't, promise me somehow, someway, even if it is only in my dreams, you'll meet me at St Brelade?

Your leprechaun,

Bobby x

'

Trying to open the impossibly jammed glass bottle, I sighed in exhaustion at my failed attempts. Failing miserably, despite having planned to launch this note along with Finns into the sea. I chose to fold the notes over and place it inside my hoody pocket, until I swapped the bottle back at home.

Talk about bad timing, my phone began to ring.

'Where are you?'

'I'm on the beach at St Brelade's, I just fancied a walk.'

'Stay where you are,' ordered Finn.

'What? Why?'

'How do you fancy Pizza on the beach; Zoe's informed me you love that Pizzeria.'

'I do and how come you finished work so early?'

'Sea is a bit choppy, so we've shut up early. So early dinner, pizza on the beach before the tide comes in, then a few beers at Odyseey bar on the sea front.'

'I'm not exactly dressed for a date, I'm in my scruffs, I should go home and change.'

'No stay as you are because were against the tide times, besides Bobby you'd look a rockstar in a bin bag. Your gorgeous!'

'Oh hurry up !'

'Why hurry? Can you not wait to lock lips with a rugged Irishman who has salt, surfed, messy hair and wrinkled hands from the ocean, because I want to see my blonde goddess.'

'No nothing to do with that, I can't wait for a slice of Margherita'.

'Nice to know I stand in firm competition with a cheesy tomato doughy....'

'Not just any pizza base of tomato sauce, we're talking mozzarella and cheddar cheese, sprinkled with oregano and black pepper drizzled in olive oil', I butted in.

'Bobby get off and stop reading the online menu!'

'How did you know?'

'I know everything', he said whilst putting down the phone.

As he ended the call laughing, I let out a cry from within and muttered, 'If only you did'.

Apart from spending the next twenty minutes or so re-reading the online menu salivating now over the desert section and snooping on holiday goers, the time passed quickly and before I knew it I spotted Finn waving frantically above the beach. Squinting my eyes not once but twice I quickly confirmed standing next to

‘

him was Corbin and Zoe in some form of an embrace. Mainly consisting of Zoe squeezing the life out of Corbin. I rolled my eyes and the sight and instantly knew Finn had turned our date into a double date, involving the two people I had tried to avoid at all costs.

Waving back, I sent Finn a text with my order and told him to tell Zoe to come down to me. Rubbing my hands together nervously with a wave of sickness and mild agitation, I repeatedly told myself to smile and focus my energy on Finn.

'Hey girly, are you feeling better?' screeched Zoe in an over hyped voice.

'Yeah, loads better, it's good to see you. This is nice.'

'I know, Finn was talking about some restaurant. I was like hell no, she loves the pizza shop at St Brelade'.

'Good shout. How's things with you and Corbin?'

'Amazing, we're talking about going to Marbella for a long weekend probably next month. Take our relationship to another level.'

'Nice, they do say it's a way to test a relationship. If you can bear a hotel room and being next to each other on holiday then you have potential to go all the way,' I smiled.

'Corbin's the one. I know it'.

'Just be careful Zoe', I added.

'Meaning?' she grunted.

'You girls ready for a feast', called Corbin.

'Yes babe, I'm starving', cooed Zoe.

'What did you mean Bobby', repeated Zoe.

'Nothing, just words', I said reassuringly.

'This was a good shout Corbin', said Finn,

'Yeah, but I will need to go for a run later. No carbs before Marbs', said Corbin.

'Marbs?' said Finn.

'This is the point where you tell Finn, he's the boss for a week', shouted Zoe.

'A week? I said a long weekend', said Corbin firmly.

'Are you going away boss?'

'Zoe's idea', he nudged Finn.

'Nice one', shrugged Finn.

'Quiet Bobby, you still rough? I bet your glad I checked on her while you were in Guernsey', scorned Corbin,

'Oh, thanks pal, you never said Bobby'.

'

'Flu fog must have slipped my mind', I said instantly regretting my choice of words.

'I'm much better now thanks Corbin. Luckily for me I also had Finn at the end of phone, he was my medicine'.

'So cute', wined Zoe.

'Who ordered pepperoni?' enquired Finn.

'That would be me', said Corbin.

'You told me you didn't eat meat unless it was a special occasion', gasped Zoe.

'Well, I guess we will call this a special occasion', wheezed Corbin through his lying teeth.

'Why is it special? Do I have a surprise?'

'Zoe hush, you'll ruin the surprise', freaked Corbin, whom I could tell was spinning yet another web of lies. Feeling sorry for my friend I came to the rescue.

'Corbin's booked you and I in for a pamper session at the L'Horizon spa. I shouldn't spoil the surprise, but a FULL day pass including lunch is something to get excited about,' I added.

'So, you were planning a surprise for me all along. I did wonder why you had called into Bobby's cottage,' beamed Zoe.

'

'Hush now and eat, before it gets cold', ordered Corbin and just like that we all halted on conversation and scoffed our delicious pizza like a pack of ravenous pride of lions.

'Who fancies a refill?' asked Corbin.

'Me', said Finn.

'Me too', added Zoe.

'Fancy giving me a hand Bobby, if you pick at the pizza anymore, it won't be worth asking for a doggy bag', scorned Corbin.

'Sure, I'll help you', I replied.

'I wish I had brought my cardigan', stuttered Zoe.

Feeling quite warm and well, heated from Corbin's behaviour, I removed my hoody and passed it Zoe.

'Aww besties for life', smiled Zoe.

I just smiled back and walked with Corbin, towards the steep steps of the beach and up towards the bar. Trying to make zero conversation with him, I just nodded and grunted to his obnoxious voice. I wasn't remotely enjoying the company or even the early evening on the beach. The only gem in the moment was the pizza which never failed to live up to its renowned reputation.

'

Chapter Twenty-One

Waiting to be served felt like an eternity. The bar was heaving mainly of tourists. Not many locals used this bar except out of season. One of the reasons why I came to love Murphy's so much, it was brimmed with us locals. We had knitted a community spirit, and we all knew each other by name. The environment was cosy and inviting.

'Drink?' enquired Corbin.

'I'll just have a bottle of cola thanks', I replied.

'You need to stop acting weird around me, before a rat is sniffed,' he ordered.

'I'm not the rat here', I gloated.

'Grow up Bobby, it's not always about you. You had your chance !'

'Chance ha, with you !' I huffed in laughter.

'Your loss'.

'I never wanted a chance with you Corbin. You're the one who needs to grow up', I said whilst walking off with my cola in hand leaving him to catch the bill.

I couldn't believe the cheek of Corbin. Even know he was still so unbelievably delusional to think, I wanted to even go there with him. Just standing next to me made my skin crawl all over.

Heading back down the steps and onto the beach I could see Zoe waving her hands around and Finn with his hands over his head. As I got closer, the warmth from his face had vanished and he was left with a pasty coating down to his chin.

'Corbin's bringing the drinks', I called out.

I could see from my left Zoe shaking her head and trying to avoid contact with my eyes.

'You, okay?' I asked Finn whilst crouching down beside him.

'So was it all by chance Bob? Or did you set out to come find me? A guy who worked by the sea. Did you try to track me down?' said Finn coldly.

'What are you talking about?' I engaged.

'This!' he threw the notes out of the bottle at me.

'How do you know about these? Where did you find these?' I panicked.

'They were in your hoody pocket. I put my hand in your pocket of the hoody you gave me to keep warm in. I was looking for a lip balm,' said Zoe hesitantly.

'Next time don't snoop Zoe. I gave you my hoody to keep warm, not organise my pockets', I bit back.

'I told him, that day we all met it was just by chance. I told him Bobby, but he will not listen.'

'Everything all right here', said the Corbin the creep.

'No, unless you call stalking surfers a cool thing to do', blurted Finn.

'Who? What? Where?' asked Corbin.

'I wrote a note before I left Ireland. I threw it in the sea. In that note, I wrote things. Personal things. Things that shouldn't have been read. Somehow, the girl I've come to fall for, knows all about it.'

'Finn, I found this a matter of hours ago. I swear. Me and you, it was all by chance how we met,' I pleaded.

'It's true Corbin,' said Zoe.

'Odd if you ask me', muttered Corbin.

'Shut up you,' I interrupted.

'The thing is pal; she has a thing for surfers. Only the other day, she made a pass at me. I told her I was committed to Zoe.'

'You liar', I screamed.

'Bobby, you tried to hook up with my bf?' bellowed Zoe.

'No, more like the other way around.'

'You and him?' said Finn.

'There is no me and Corbin,' I shouted.

'I trusted you Bob, I thought you were different. You know, your letter back to me, makes out for a good read. Believable I give you that.'

'You weren't meant to read it,' I shed a tear.

'Going to throw it in the ocean, was you?' Asked Finn.

'Yes, I was actually. I thought if I wrote back and sealed the notes together then somehow, I would have set you free.'

'I'm not some caged bird', he said sharply.

'I think you've swerved a bomb here pal,' mumbled Corbin.

'Do I not even get a sorry here? When were you going to tell me?' asked Zoe.

'Hush Zoe, the world doesn't revolve around you. Hurry up and learn that Barbie', scorned Corbin.

'How dare you! I'm done', Zoe walked off in temper.

Corbin huffed and rubbed his head in regret at speaking to Zoe in such an uncouth manner.

'Zoe wait up, I didn't mean that', he said whilst running after her.

'

'Nothing happened Finn. Corbin tried to kiss me; he turned up unexpectedly, he forced himself on me', I pleaded.

'Course he did Bobby', he added.

'Hello Bobby', I heard a voice form behind.

'Agnes!' I chocked.

'Hello dear, is this Finley? I've heard so much about you,' she smiled.

I couldn't help but think bad timing. I was in a full-blown argument come confrontation with Finn. Now just wasn't a good time.

'How'd you do?' smiled Finn standing up to shake Agnes' hand.

'You have strong hands', she cooed.

'I happened to have heard a great deal about you to Agnes. Bobby has been telling me how she's been keeping you company.'

'Oh yes, lovely Bobby. You know I spent a wonderful few hours at the cottage, I also met your boss, well I saw him giving it all large in the kitchen'.

'Is that so', he replied.

'I have rather a bad headache Agnes, you will have to excuse me, I need to go close my eyes.'

'Oh dear, can I give you an aspirin?'

'I'm okay, can I give you a ride back home or drop you off anywhere Agnes'.

'Oh, I'm okay dear, I'm meeting my next-door neighbour here any moment,' she said.

'Okay, I'll see you soon Agnes. Finn?'

'Not now Bobby. I'm going to stay here for a while. I think you've said all there is to say.'

'I'll keep him company till my neighbour comes', insisted Agnes.

Turning and walking away from both Agnes and Finn, felt wrong, and weird considering I had come to be fond and make connections with both of them. I could see though from turning my head back, Agnes in full conversation with Finn. I did chuckle, I'm sure she would have loved all the attention Finn was giving her. I felt so angry and upset at the same time. How could Corbin tell such lies, such a fabrication of facts. The way both Zoe and Finn looked at me, was crushing. Not one part of it was truth. I knew my gut instinct had turned out to be right about Corbin. Evidently his good looks and charm, masked his vulgar and scheming personality. Then there was the letter, how could I have been so foolish to have not realised the note was in my hoody pocket.

That's kindness for you. You do a good deed in lending your hoody to a friend and get a explosion in return. I felt relieved to some extent that Finn knew, but there was no hope in making him believe me, especially after Corbin's admission to the argument. That nugget only added petrol to the already burning fire.

I found it odd how one minute you can be on cloud nine and the next, well I can't even think of a word to use, but I'm sure you feel me. I needed the comforting feeling of being within the walls of my little cottage. Safe and hidden away from everything and everyone. I had spent pretty much the day breaking my heart, feeling emotions which were rootbound, deep in a tangled mess. I had tried to repot and sprinkle my bean of compost into the mix, thinking it would bloom a new beginning. How I was wrong.

I wept tears of sadness, tear of joy and tears over what could have been. What I had with Finn, felt so real and alive, if I could fly, I had been soaring well above the clouds and heading out of the universe. That's how I had come to feel with Finn, his existence had become my very own universe and the two of us together was going on a space voyage of dreams.

I unlocked my phone screen; to see a photo of Finn and I ask my background. I kissed my fingertip and draped my finger over his face.

'Oh Finn, if only you knew the truth', I sighed.

With itchy fingers I penned a text and erased it. Then I tried again and back tracked it halfway through. I shook my head in disbelief. No text was going to cut what I had to say. I pushed the dial button down to call Finn. Yep, you've guessed it. I got sent to voicemail. Maybe he had no service I told myself.

'Finn, I want you to know, there is no truth in what Corbin had to say down at the beach. I don't know how you'll ever believe me or how I can try make you believe that. I am telling you the truth though. As for the letter. I never set out to find the guy behind the note. We were already a thing. I just knew when I found it, it was you who had written it. I didn't know what to do. I was scared to tell you in case this happened,' I paused gulping for air as my mouth had dried out. 'Finn, I'm sorry. I'm sorry for just about everything I can be sorry for. Well, that's not exactly true. I won't be sorry for meeting you. Meeting you was the best thing to ever happened to me. As for the note in the bottle, it only showed me a side of you, I was yet to learn about. A side of you which made me realise, I might think I have it all, a postcode in Jersey, a cottage of dreams nestled by the sea, true friendships, a job which keeps me clothed in all the fast fashion a girl could dream of. Yet, those only are materialistic. What's the point in the JE post code, the job, the clothes, and the cottage by the sea without you

by my side. It pointless, it's like having a clock without a battery, you wouldn't know the time. I choose to want to know the time, and spend my time on this earth, making each and every hour count. I made a commitment not so long ago to find out what the meaning of an hour meant. I'm not prepared to stop exploring that. The reason why is because that hour brought me to you. My very own Irish blessing.'

Placing down my phone, I broke down in a crumpled heap on the floor, with no strength in my legs to attempt to re-stand. My world around me had collapsed. I had no value to my name. I was just Bobby, a tragic fool, who only chose to believe and dabble in a little 'Draiocht'- (the correct term for a little, traditional Irish magic).

Chapter Twenty-Two

Weeks had gone by and just like the sailboat in my morning view, I had been left, washed out at the peak of tide. Those weeks turned themselves into months and the summer had flashed before my eyes. For the first few days since I had left Finn that voicemail, I would check my phone for texts and e-mails on the hour. When that brought me no joy, I turned to scan my socials and stalk Finn's. My heart sank at first when he tagged his location back in Ireland but as the days passed and the uploads of horses and horse eventing became Finn's feed. I came to accept he had left Jersey and returned home. The tears came and left, then returned whenever they felt like messing up my eye makeup.

As for Zoe, she had to learn the hard way about Corbin. Of course, I was there to heal the pain she felt. Zoe had apologised over and over to me for not essentially believing me. I chose not to hold a grudge; I just let it go. I knew only too well what it felt like to be head over heels in love. If anything, mine and Zoe's friendship had grown an extra dimension, and I was very much back in the role of wing woman. Zoe as expected had moved on and was now romancing

'

Jacob of all people. Worked in my favour though as we got a good discount at Murphy's. To have two of my closest friends now a couple, was cute but sometimes I was for sure a gooseberry sandwich between the two.

I had chosen to throw myself in the deep end of work. So much so, you're now talking to a trainee legal receptionist. The distraction had proved beneficial as I had even managed to get a pay rise, which helped with the bills. I was also gifted some time out of the week to study law at the local college, to gain more knowledge into the legal world. I was proud of my achievements and reassured to know I was making a career path for myself in this world.

Between being a gooseberry and working my derriere off, I had also managed to redecorate my kitchen. With the help of both Zoe and Jacob and even Agnes, I now had a buttermilk yellow kitchen, to wake me up each morning. The colour wasn't my first choice it was Agnes' preference, so allowing her to guide me, it was safe to say she had chosen well. Sunshine yellow I had chosen to re-name it. Who would have thought a change of colour to the walls had encouraged me to cook a lot healthier and from scratch too.

Despite still owning a burning hole in my heart, I had somehow grown as an individual in just about everyway a woman could be allowed to grow. I often played back that scenario on the beach. I chose to rewind it and pretend in my mind the whole argument had changed a direction. Doing that didn't help but it was my minds way of processing it still. I never found out what Finn and Agnes had talked about when I left. I didn't want to pry.

With summer now collapsed into early autumn, most of the holiday makers had vanished and our beautiful island of Jersey, which we had shared with tourists had near enough returned to its fellow Islanders. I like to think of us residents as the power troops who keep the magic of Jersey alive in the autumn/winter months.

Knowing that the last of the flowers were waving there gentle goodbye and the heat from the summer sun was warming the waters for the last time, made my heart crush from within. Summer on Jersey is like no other. The endless days, the long nights, the suns presence kissing our skin. Summers on Jersey were dreamy. Not this one though, it had started with every intention to be the best yet, but somehow, the sand had sieved it's way through my fingertips leaving an emptiness, which was cold and unsettling.

Seeing the leaves turn amber and wither as they fell, was a treat. Summer for sure had waved its last goodbye, taking a piece of my heart away with it, leaving a rug of leaves, I needed to begin to sweep.

'

However much I had distracted myself, those screens only provided a temporary faze. The thought of autumn turning into winter, filled me with dismay. The idea of spending those long, dark evening alone made my inner spirit nervous. I felt so lost. The worst was, I was now experiencing what it was like to bottle my feelings up. I was present in life but waiting to burst and essentially flip my lid.

'Are you ready?' smiled Zoe.

'No, I'm not coming Zoe. I think I'll sit and watch the air display here'.

'Come on, it will be fun,' she pushed.

'No honestly, I just want to be alone.'

'Okay. You will be okay you know,' Zoe said with encouragement.

'I know, I just cant help but wonder what Finn's up to.'

'Well stop wondering, he's not worth it Bobby. He is the only eigit,' she laughed attempting her best irish accent to say the word idiot.

'Oh don't, I can't bear to hear that accent.'

'You know where to find Jacob and I, if you change your mind,' she smiled whilst leaning over to hug me.

Zoe had been staying at my house quite a lot over the last few weeks. Normally I would find her irritating and wouldn't recommend we lived out of each other's pockets as Zoe was quite hyperactive, but somehow, she had been a perfect friend to me.

Today was the Battle of Britain Air Display or as some chose to call it the Jersey Air display. Wizardry in the sky I would call it. To see such beautiful and magnificent aircrafts in the sky was a sight to savour. Jersey had come so far from the once Island which ached under occupation. Now to see the likes, of the Red Arrows, The Navy Blackcats and my personal favourite the Typhoon in our skies, high above our gentle waters was a moment of celebration. I had planned to watch the spectacle from the comfort of my garden, surrounded by the last of my flowers and cosy sherpa blanket for added warmth. To be lazy, I even planned on making a flask of hot tea. To move or take your eyes away from the sky could be disastrous in missing the aircrafts.

I made the effort and wondered into my room and warmed the barrel on my curling tongs. The once blonder than blonde highlight had now turned into my natural chocolate regrowth. I didn't have the want to have them touched up. I enjoyed seeing some richness to my hair which left the strand ends blessed with a reminder of the summer that was. I guess everything has to come to an end in some way, shape or form.

Sectioning of my hair, I created some soft waves, alternating each curl in a different direction to give that voluminous look. I chose to curl the front sections away from my face, to give a softer appearance. I think if you ask any woman, having her hair done, gives you such a good feeling from within. To be frank, I am happy to go out with little to no makeup providing my hair is looking good. Giving each curl a gentle tease and spraying it with copious amounts of hairspray, the job was done to perfection. I think Kyle would be proud. I must mention here that he now too has gone solo on his hairdressing adventure and rents a shop in the indoor market. My friendship group despite small, well countable on both hands, they were all treasures in their own individual ways. I was lucky.

Pulling on my trustee band hoody, which needed sowing on the forearm, I chose to wear a cute white ra-ra skirt, to complete the look. These pins of mine were truly mini skirt worthy, and soon, let's face it, it will be too cold to get them out. Slipping on my shearling booties, and collecting my mini-imaginary picnic which was just a flask and pack of custard creams from Marks' in town (if you know, you know. They are the best). I made my way to the garden table and set up my seating area, and wrapped my shearling blanket around me,

The sky was the perfect conditions to watch the planes above. I was glad I had chosen to stay at home. I intended and told my mind strictly, I was going to enjoy today and not think of you know who.

The perfect day, calmness all around with the warmth of Channel Island sun, smiling down on me. Today Bobby is the day, your are going to put summer well behind you. I have to be strong. I have to steal some of that Jersey solidarity and strength, my island showed all those years ago and inhabit it into my life.

Today was the day, I was going to end the war in my head, the constant battle with my mind over Finn. I was no longer going to be the girl, on the island at war.

I was Bobby, from St Brelade. I was made of tough stuff, just like my beautiful island of Jersey.

Chapter Twenty-Two

The sight of the Typhoon took my breath away and partially burst my ear drums at that. What a machine capable of supersonic speeds made of such a fragile streamlined construction. I loved aviation. The roar of the flypast filled my bones with adrenaline. Truly marvellous. We are lucky to have such planes as part of our military. Seeing them in the skies was a delight.

Next was the aerobatic team. Admittedly, I don't know how these peoples held their stomachs. I couldn't do what they do. Loops and spins, twists and turns, I have enough on the bumper cars. Looking up and over to my right I could see a pale blue plane in sight, flying at steep angle, attempting a loop, billowing out its pretty shades of rainbow smoke. The sky was a sight. Joined closely by an orange plane, they both began to weave in between one another, creating shapes and patterns in the sky. The odd release of a few parachutes decorated the sky, as though rain was trinkling down towards the ocean. The smile on my face, began to ache my cheek bones and I couldn't remove my eyes from the skyline. That's when a small plane, which didn't appear to look like it had the ability to perform any acrobats, flew across the sky and then banked and swooped its way towards the middle of the skyline.

'

The acrobatic planes now pluming out pink smoke from their canisters was so pretty and cute, if planes can even be described as cute. Trust me on this, the sky just looked so feminine against the twinkles of the sun beaming down in the diamond flecks of light which rested on the seas, calm surface.

'No way, it can't be', I gasped, cupping my hands over my cheeks, in disbelief.

'It can't be', I whispered.

Before my eyes, that small, light weight aircraft was waving a long, white ribbon sign from its tail. The word's *'Meet me at St Brelade'* printed in red.

Those words. They were my words. My plea. The word's I left on that letter I wrote to stuff into the bottle. I had asked Finn, to meet me there, if it couldn't be for real then only in my dreams. I asked my love, to meet me at St Brelade.

There was no way, that those words, could mean anything to anyone other than me. The tears began to tickle my eyelids until they rolled and streamed down my face. Those words meant just one thing.

My love was my back. My Finley. My Irish pot of gold.

With my cheeks smeared in the eyeliner and mascara. I used the damp splodges from my tears to try wipe 'away the mess, I had created on my face. Throwing my hair upside down and adding a little touch more of hair spray, I ran back outside towards the garden and down the little private access steps to the beach.

St Brelade's was abnormally quiet as most the action from the air display crowds was over at St Ouen beach. Looking from left to right frantically trying to see if my eyes hadn't tricked me. I scoured up and down the beach looking for Finn. My heart thudding inside and feeling a little short of breath and rather lightheaded, I continued to run down the beach looking for Finn. Stopping briefly and bending over to catch my breath.

That's when a familiar voice, began to speak, confirming my hopes. The voice was Finn's.

'Bobby', he tapped my shoulder and grabbed my hand and squoze it as tightly as possible.

Turning around the blubbing, tearful mess I was, I looked up and smiled, 'You came back'.

'Yeah', he sighed barely able to speak. It was evident that Finn to was chocked for words. Instead of speaking I nodded and bit my lip with nerves, at standing in front of Finn.

'I had everything planned, I was going to say, and now its…'he blurted and lost his pace.

'Say nothing, just hold me', I leapt forward into his muscular, arms.

If time could be held still, it did in that moment. I held Finn so tight and nestled my face into his shoulders. I felt safe, secure and in essence rescued. It was at that point I just knew, however much I had tried to move on with life and put my breakup with Finn aside, those deep feelings were never going to shift. I cared more than I allowed my mind to accept.

'I couldn't do it Bobby', he whispered.

'Do what?'

'Life, without you by my side,' he added and kissed my hand.

'I missed you so much Finn, you need to listen, I swear I only found that note when I said I did. I never set out to find the guy behind the note, you must believe me.'

'I do. I know all that rubbish with Corbin was all on him.'

'He told the truth?' I gasped.

'No, that fairy God Mother of yours did.'

'Agnes?' I enquired.

'Yeah'.

'You believe her, right?'

'

'Yes.'

Finn nodded and looked away towards the sea, barely able to string another sentence he was overcome with emotion.

'This place, it changes you. There's something in those waters you know,' he exclaimed.

'What do you mean?'

'The sea never fails to amaze me, Bobby. From sunrise through to daybreak, golden hour to sundown, its presence is always profound and guaranteed. If you stop and think about it, that note was always going to wash up here, on these sandy shores,' he paused allowing a tear to trickle down his cheek, not afraid to show his vulnerable nature, he never wiped it away. 'I didn't choose to come back, just because I knew the truth. I came back because, that sea, it runs through my veins. Just like the sea, I want to be by your side, come dawn through to dusk. I want my love for you to flow through to your heart and like the sea be always present and everlasting.'

Gasping in a bubble of air, I was whisked into a moment only a Disney Princess, ever gets to experience. Every word was crafted with love.

'I love you Finn', I blurted.

'I love you too Bobby,' he smiled and kissed me once more.

Smiling hand in hand, and looking out towards the sea, which was swishing and swooshing across the bay, my heart felt complete. I knew deep down, with Finn by my side life was going to be just fine.

'You know that Irish blessing about making the hour count?' he asked.

'Aye, I do', I said in my best attempt an Irish accent.

'Well, say you will be my leprechaun and instead of making just an hour count, say you'll fulfil the hour through the days and years to come?' Finn, smiled and knelt down onto one knee.

'Bobby, marry me?'

'Yes', I shrieked and collapsed in his arms. Not just any arms, the arms of someone I knew would protect me, love me and be my shelter from any storm. The arms of my Finn. My Irish pot of gold.

Two Years Later

....

'Kyle, are you sure these curls will hold?'

'Yes Bobby'.

'How are the bridesmaids looking?'

'A vision', smiled Zoe.

'Have the flowers arrived?'

'Yes Bobby, calm down and have a drink!' said Jacob.

'I told you adding those money pieces at the front of your hair would look amazing,' added Kyle.

'Well, let's face it Kyle, this hair isn't going to cram anymore highlights in', I exclaimed.

'You truly are a blonde goddess', he laughed.

'Are you nervous?' asked Zoe.

'No, surprisingly not, I have waited for this day my entire life.'

'Well, you need to get that frock on prompto, you have a wedding to get to!' ordered Kyle.

With the help of my very own crew, I stepped into my bespoke, white gown. Draped in lace and embellished with pearls around the waistline and iridescent sequins in the shapes of roses on the skirt. The dress was magnificent. Not to forget to mention the back details, instead of buttons, my dress was fastened by shells collected from each and every bay of Jersey. How could I not, include this Island of Jersey on a day which would etch with me for the rest of my life. Staring into the mirror smiling, I looked so beautiful, in every way a woman could be, my eyes sparkled, my skin glowed and I radiated happiness. I was ready, to marry my love.

Life had changed so much within the last couple of years, and here I was, standing in the most beautiful dress, about to marry the man who had taught me what love and how to love was all about. Agnes had agreed to walk me down the aisle and give me away, dressed in pale lemon and bursting with pride, she was ready for the job in hand. As for my bridesmaids dressed in pale blue, and the groom's side in marine navy, our wedding mirrored the sea, enveloping its credentials to make our special day flow, be present and everlasting.

Standing in the fisherman's chapel, at St Brelade's Bay, and looking in the eyes of my Irishman, I said those all-important words,

'I do'.

Those words in essence broke Finn's letter into pieces.

The waters of Jersey had travelled Finn's heart to mine. We were now husband and wife and about to start our own adventure, in our 'cosy Irish' cottage nestled in the bay of St Brelade, on the magical Island which had blessed me eternally. The Island of Jersey.

…. Before I go on this adventure of a lifetime…. Be sure to promise me you'll visit Jersey, the Island where dreams really do, come true.

Acknowledgments

You ask why Jersey?

Well, Jersey was the place my barely six-month-old tiny feet, first felt the sand and where my newborn skin was kissed by the warmth of the sun. Jersey had my heart from such a young age, annually implanting a seed of love, which grew throughout my childhood. I was fortunate enough to have parents that provided a holiday to visit the island three to four times a year. In fact, if I'm very honest with you, the whole adventure began from my grandparents taking my mother there when she too was just an infant. My grandfather worked day and night on the railways so he could take my mom to Jersey for two weeks every year. Back in those days, a fortnights holiday to Jersey was quite something. Then my parents, fell in love with the Island and passed the addiction and love to me.

I wish I could thank every aspect of the Island, for filling my own heart with such memories. I wouldn't be able to mention every place I had visited on the Island as this section would be never ending. However, I feel compelled to mention a few.

The hotels I stayed in, ranged from the Merton Hotel, and the splendour of the Aquadome. The number of times I have slid down that magic slide is uncountable, not to forget the outdoor mushroom of showers. The staff, Donald the waiter who waited on us year in year out. The Jersey Joe, milkshakes which deserve recognition in their own right. The star room, to be entertained and the games room to spend Dad's money on the Air hockey machine. The twin receptionists, Sinead and Dee who greeted us with smiles. Then there was the Irish Lifeguard who I took a liking too, giving me a tennis ball and scribbling all over it his name and a heart on our first meeting. Yes, I still own that tennis ball. You were the guy, whom I based Finn on. I don't know where you live now, or if you are even still in Jersey, but your Irish accent did melt my heart and allowed me to create Finn's character. So, in a way, I will say Thank you. The Merton Hotel, you allowed me to make memories that I will treasure forever.

Then there is the Hotel L'Horizon, the hotel that allowed me to fall in love with the bay of St Brelade, on a unimaginable scale. Dad with the pressure of his businesses, very much needed this hotel, to relax and switch off. It's thanks to my mom and him; we had the opportunity to holiday in Jersey so frequently. L'Horizon Hotel, thank you for allowing me to rest my head on the most comfortable pillows. To wake up and pull back your curtains, to the sights and sounds of St Brelade, those feelings, imprinted my heart. The kind staff, the delicious food and relaxing Spa. Pure bliss.

Then there are the special attractions on the Island. I will be sure to mention a few, The Jersey Zoo, just an incredible day out, of laughter and fun. The work that goes into the Zoo and the Durrell Wildlife Conservation Trust is magnificent. I am a huge animal lover and to see the animals, so cared for and protected is truly beautiful. A visit is a must and any form of donation I'm sure would be greatly appreciated.

The Jersey War Tunnels, an opportunity to understand and feel the strength of the Island during the German occupation. The tunnels, will have the hairs on your arms stand on end, and you will feel emotions you never knew existed within you. Each and every time I have visited, I've left learning new facts.

The Jersey Pearl, St Ouen- This Jewellery company, began my love and addiction to pearls. Every year, come Christmas I treat myself to a piece of Jewellery from here. I know have quite a beautiful collection, with each wear, I always feel close to the Island. Not to mention, the food again, is ten ten.

Elizabeth Castle and Gorey Castle- To understand what it feels like to be royalty looking over your land and sea, is a grand feeling. I experienced this when I first visited these beautiful historical buildings. No words can sum up these visits other than, you would be missing out by not visiting them.

Then to keep this huge list short, I'll throw in a few extra's which I truly recommend- The Portelet Inn and the Old Smugglers Inn (both exceptional food and a feeling of cosiness and history fill the walls).

La Corbiere Lighthouse (an ice-cream here is a must).

Portelet beach (you need to feel the burn from the steps down to the beach) when you get there, your heart will melt at such a treasure of a beach.

St.Helier, a town filled with locals, cafés and home to the indoor market. Not to forget- be sure to visit, De Gruchy and Voisins, a purchase is a must, you need to feel the thrill of swinging that carrier bag down King Street. It totally takes the word boujee to a new level.

Bergerac – The British crime drama that ran through the eighties. I do not know the number of times of heard this famous theme tune on our tv at home growing up. The number of times I have stood by Jim Bergerac's car for a photo as a child for a photo opportunity. What a programme though! It's wonderful that such great people have re-booted the drama. Also, if you have not heard it you need to play the remastered edition of Bergerac by Youngr- that song makes me cry every time I watch the video on YouTube! What a song!

The Bambola Toymaster- this shop was where I can recall and have very fond memories of buying my

Barbie 1997 Holiday collectors' doll with my holiday spending money, along with my sibling buying a huge stuffed animal, which filled the seat of our Saab convertible. I also recall my mother buying the cassette of the single Ultra Nate Free song from Woolworths. Then causing some damage playing the record, roof down, dad driving along the esplanade. A day I will never forget.

Overall, my thanks go to Jersey, the island itself.

Jersey, you have my heart, from the moment my feet first touched the ground. I cannot express my love for the Island. There isn't a stone I don't think I've not uncovered here. Every bay, every landmark, every building, all means something to someone in Jersey. The history of the Island and how it displayed such heroism, in such testing times during the Nazi Occupation, is inspiring. The warmth of the Jersey people, so kind, so patient and so happy.

Jersey, what more can I say, you captured and stole my heart.

♡